# Out of the Blue

## Short Stories

# Eddie Stack

A Tintaun Original

Tintaun

25 Berkeley Way
San Francisco, CA 9413

Ballylara Cottage
Labane, Ardrahan
Co Galway, Ireland

www.tintaun.com

"Angels" was first published in *Fiction* (USA)

"Out of the Blue" first appeared in *Confrontation* (USA)

"Dreamin' Dreams" was previously published in *Island Online* (www.iaf.org)

"Waiting for a Fare," "Back in the Days of Corncrakes"

and "Journeymen" were all previously

published in the *Clare Champion* (Ireland)

ISBN 1-930579-13-6

Library of Congress Control Number: 2003110488

Published in the United States of America
First Edition, 2004

design: Bill Roarty
cover design: Mary Gaynor

*for*
*Jimmy Stack*

# CONTENTS

# Out of the Blue

Eddie Stack

# ANGELS

ONE BALMY EVENING, JUST BEFORE THE SUN sank behind the roof-tops, Aggie Lally scurried across the street and disappeared into Hogan's Drapery.

"Is there someone dead?" she asked Mariah, "There's a lot of people in the street—like they're waiting for a funeral or something."

Mariah hadn't noticed and poked her permed head out the door. Up and down the town, bunches of townsfolk stood around shops and corners; more criss-crossed the road to each other's houses, often meeting halfway. The town buzzed.

"What's happening?" Aggie asked urgently.

"God, I don't know," whispered Mariah.

Aggie tilted her head, sniffed the air like a fox and said,

"But 'tis very odd isn't it? Even peculiar. I wonder if the lads across the street know anything about it?"

Bold as a sparrow, she flitted over to Coleman's Corner where Paddy Logan held court with James Dillon and Coyne the Butcher.

"How're ye men—what's happenin' at all? Is there some big shot comin' to town or what?"

They shrugged and Coyne spat into the gutter.

"God but 'tis very strange, isn't it? Hah?" said Dillon, squinting up Church Street at a few groups scattered outside pubs. Now a crowd gathered around the post office.

"An' there's no funeral from America that we don't know about?" pressed Aggie.

Coyne pursed his lips and shook his head, he hated to be in the dark.

"I'll take a stroll down the street," he muttered, "I'll see ye again in a while."

He wondered what the crowd at Hartigan's Corner were chattering about and headed their way. They gazed across the street at Hanlon's Radio and Bicycle Shop. Years closed and shuttered, it had gone unnoticed until now; even Coyne had forgotten about it. Coming closer, he got excited and shouted that he saw flames leaping through the roof. No, the gazers said, it was only the setting sun dancing off the skylight. 'Another smart man fooled,' someone muttered and they stamped their feet and doubled up laughing.

"Fuck ye!" the butcher grunted and slunk around the corner to Clare Street. He threw back his shoulders, straightened the peak of his cap and marched up to the police barracks.

"Malone will know what's happening," he muttered and clenched his fists at the thought of going back to the corner blaggards with the news.

He rapped urgently on the barracks door. Hollow as a tomb. No reply. He knocked again, louder this time, and called,

"Sergeant! Con Coyne here."

"Empty box!" a woman yelled from the far side of the street: Gretta Green, the mad woman from Frowhell.

"Empty box! He's gone to the races," she shouted, "Ridin' mad. The whole country's ridin' mad. What d'you want 'im for? Hah?"

Coyne ignored her, but she kept shouting, turning heads, attracting attention to the butcher who stood facing the barracks like a brooding bull.

Gretta was getting louder, coming closer, ragging him. Coyne's blood was on the boil and he wanted to bawl at her and wring her neck like he did with chickens and turkeys.

"He won't be back till Saturday," she rattled, "don't you see the notice in the window?"

Coyne's fists twitched but he checked them,

"Gretta," he said gruffly, "why don't you fuck off home like a good girl?"

"Fuck off yourself, you ram you. The law is gone. There's no law in town. D'you hear me? Ridin'. He's gone ridin'."

At that very moment the street below erupted in cheers and the butcher jolted with confusion, wondering if he was the root of the joke. But the cheers were for Roddy's red lorry, rumbling into town with a gang of road-swept county council workers. Before the wagon stopped in the square, hundreds swarmed around it, scouring for news. Oddly, the oil-skinned workers had none and said nothing was happening up the country. All was quiet on the western front. Roddy stuck his bullet head out of the cab and said he overheard one of the road engineers say there was trouble in China.

"Would that have anything to do with it?" Mariah asked Aggie Lally.

"China?" chirped Aggie, "China? Is that where Father Murphy is with the foreign missions?"

Mariah shook her head and blurted,

"I don't know...but Jesus Mary 'n Joseph...Aggie, is that Harry Fine the Chemist that I see?"

Aggie blessed herself and clutched Mariah by the elbow.

"Sweet Heart of Jesus," she muttered, "I can't believe my eyes."

Across the street, Mr. Fine the reclusive chemist stood at the hall door of his green shuttered shop, in white tennis clothes and boater hat. Nobody had seen him for years, though they heard him play the violin every once in a while. Now children flocked around him and grown-ups shook his hand and asked how he was. Fine, he said, just fine. He praised the weather and said it was just like the summer evenings of long, long ago when Morgan Dunphy and himself played tennis on the grass court behind Riverview Lodge.

"Crikey," he said, stepping out on the footpath a few feet "but it's great to be alive."

Mr. Fine looked up to heaven,

"Listen to the birds below in the wood," he urged quietly, and his well-wishers did. Blackbirds, thrushes, linnets and finches of every strain sang their hearts out and nobody missed Mr. Fine until he re-appeared at an upstairs window, violin in hand, tenderly crooning,

"The gay flowers are shining, gilt o'er by the sun,

But the fairest of all is my own Molly Dunne."

Mariah Hogan thought it was the most moving verse she had heard in years and wanted to throw flowers at the singer, the eccentric man she had long ago fallen in and out of love with. And nobody knew. Not even Mr. Fine, who could never remember her name no matter how many times she came to his Medical Hall with aches and pains for the curing.

When Mariah sighed back to the present, the town teemed with children of all ages, some spinning timber tops, others rolling bicycle wheels up the middle of the road, more played colored glass marbles on the footpath. In the space of a few minutes it seemed they had popped out of the ground like daisies. In all her life Mariah had never seen so many children, sporting and playing and running rings around grown-ups.

By twilight a troop of young ruffians had gathered turf and timber, tires and other things burnable, and set about building a huge bonfire in the square. Coyne the butcher was on hand to lend advice and called on everyone to give more fuel.

"Pile it on," he shouted, "the more the merrier."

Aggie Lally clutched Mariah, raised her eyes to heaven and whispered,

"Has the bloody butcher gone soft in the head?"

Mariah said he'd been bats for years, and told her a story she had never uttered to another soul, about a love letter the butcher once wrote her. It was straight out of dirty book, she said and quoted it at length.

"Jesus Christ," panted Aggie, "I'll never be able to look at another piece of meat again, after hearing that."

The bonfire grew and grew from the ground like a big cone and Mattie Kelly, by now drunk as a lord, announced it was going to be the biggest and brightest blaze the town had ever seen, and it had seen many. Waving a box of matches and a bottle of stout, he followed Coyne around the pyre as the butcher doused turf, tires and timber with oil and kerosene. A few troublemakers urged Mattie to put a match to the pile.

"Torch it Mattie! Torch it!" they shouted.

Then the question arose amongst the crowd about who should set the bonfire alight and names of this one and that floated about: Mr. Fine the reclusive chemist; The Cowboy Clancy; Jango Ryan. The butcher ignored the suggestions and twisted a long taper from a sheet of newspaper. He asked Mattie for the matches and bent low for shelter to light the fuse. Match after match cracked but none sparked. Coyne swore at Mattie and shouted for another box of matches. The crowd mooed and the butcher grew restless.

"Matches!" he shouted clicking his fingers, "Matches! Matches! Quick for fuck's sake!"

Too late. He smelled smoke, oily smoke, and then a gush of flame rushed around the bonfire, chased by Gretta Greene, his nightmare. Coyne went wild and swore like a man possessed by demons. He swore at Gretta, swore at Mattie Kelly and swore at the crowd until he was hoarse and demented. When he began frothing at the mouth, demanding fight and punching his fists at midges, Paddy Hogan grabbed him by the elbow and led him home. The crowd rumbled and shook their heads. Gretta Greene raced around them and rattled,

"He ate too much mate. Botta-botta. Red mate. Botta-botta."

Soon the fire was crackling and sparks and smoke funnelled high into the night. Mattie Kelly staggered around the blaze clapping his hands and shouting,

"Music! Music! Where's the music!?!"

And then above the noise of the fire came strains of violin music and Mr. Fine, pale as a ghost strolled from the smokey shadows crooning,

"Oft in the stilly night..."

It was chillingly beautiful and became more so when Angie Kelly, the church organist harmonized in the chorus. Aggie and Mariah whimpered along and soon the town hummed. It was a musical fit for Broadway: Mr. Fine strolling slowly, crooning softly, stroking his violin; Angie Kelly singing harmonies and everyone else humming like Hollywood extras, swaying with the blaze. It was a beautiful night, tranquil as the first Christmas.

Everything was heavenly and harmonious until about halfway through the song, when Gretta Green threw herself to the ground. She pulled her skirt up over her head and screamed that she had seen angels dancing in the flames of the bonfire. The singing faltered. Then Nora Flanagan noticed them, three angels with long golden wings and small harps, twirling in the flames like a carousel. Nora slumped to her knees, hands joined in prayer. And then Mattie Kelly gasped,

"Oh Holy mother of Jesus."

He saw them too, and collapsed in a bundle.

The music stopped and the three angels vanished. A couple of men helped Nora and Gretta to their feet and Strike Hogan gave them cigarettes. Mattie was revived but refused to go home, he raved about the angels and wept over their beauty. Nora nodded. She had never seen such handsome creatures, sensuous and sacred. Seeing them smile was worth all the tea in China. Gretta was in deep shock. Speechless. Trembling. The word went around, quick as lightening—

"They're after seeing an apparition."

To hold the vision, Angie Kelly burst into a hymn and those who knew it joined in. The crowd gathered closer to the fire, scanning the flames for the angels and throwing anxious glances at Nora, Gretta and Mattie. Dead pan faces. No angels. Wrong song, Mattie whispered.

Lala Lynch tried "When Irish Eyes are Smiling" and everyone sang along, eyes on the flames, eyes on the watchers. No angels. "South of the Border" was rendered next by Dilly Gillespie and her brother Tom the Albino. Still no angels. It was all in their minds, the crowd began to murmur. And then Mr. Fine played a haunting air on the violin and began to croon,

"My Love is a Red, Red Rose..."

Angie Kelly joined in the chorus, breasts heaving, and when the song built up steam, Gretta saw the angels again and Nora did too. Mattie Kelly burst into tears and moaned,

"Oh dear Jesus, there they are...three of them."

A few more saw the angels and people craned their necks and squinted at the flames. Henry Hennesy fainted when he spotted them and so did his wife Dodo. The Gallagher sisters saw them too, as did Martin Mack and Mary, Nan Lang, Aggie and Mariah.

As more and more saw the vision, there was a ripple of hysteria and Jack Webster, the retired policeman, ran to his car and booted up the hill to inform Father White.

The priest was alarmed. An apparition below in the square? Three angels dancing in the flames of the bonfire? Are you sure they're angels Jack? Who saw them? Anyone else, Jack?

"Henry Hennesy and Dodo."

"Oh my God!"

Father White grabbed his kit and Jack briefed him in the car. At the square, the priest was flabbergasted by the antics of his flock.

"Dear God," he whispered and Jack nodded.

It was disturbing. Pagan. The crowd were singing, those who

weren't praying or crying or hugging each other. Paddy Keane, a pillar of both church and society, prayed hysterically to the flames, hands outstretched like Jesus. Even the unmarried mother with the two little brats who lived in the flat over the bakery was on her knees, head bowed in holy devotion.

Father White gaped at the fire but saw no angels. He walked around it, squinting from different places. No angels. The town is in a trance, he thought and his skin tightened when he noticed some lunatic distributing candles. Hundreds of tiny flames quivered to light and the square began to look like a U2 concert. Father White sweated and waved his hands,

"Stop! Stop! Stop!" he yelled, "Stop this idolatry!"

But nobody listened to him, not even Larry Prise nor Mary Getty, Paddy Foley or Biddy Bailey—the most faithful of the Faithful. Not even his own church organist, Angie Kelly. Jack Webster was at his side—right hand man. Webster saw no angels either and muttered,

"It's something they drank. They're all gaga."

Father White nodded rapidly, "They're hallucinating," he blurted, "I see it in their eyes."

Mr. Fine, who Father White had never seen before, strolled amongst the idolators with a smile as big as a horseshoe, playing a medley of waltzes on the violin. Jack Webster nudged the priest,

"He's a chemist, I bet he has something to do with it."

The priest jerked his head like a dog spotting a cat. A chemist playing the devil's instrument! He waded through the crowd after the violinist, calling,

"Hello! Excuse me!"

He gained on Mr. Fine, tapped him on the shoulder and when the chemist turned around, Father White grabbed his fiddle and pitched it at the bonfire. It was a long, slow throw and the fiddle somersaulted head over heel, higher and higher above the fire. It hovered there for a minute or two, and then tumbled, majestic as a high diver, into the smoke and the sparks and the orangey-blue tongues of flame. Time stood still, everyone stood still, watching entranced as the fiddle fell slower than a snowflake, into the fire where minutes before, the angels had been. And then Gretta Green screamed. She saw a face in the flames. It was Mr. Fine. The square screamed. The chemist was in the belly of the fire.

Cool as a breeze, Harry Fine plucked his fiddle from its fall and walked out of the fire unscathed. His tennis gear was virgin white, not even a smut stain on his boater hat. People gathered around him in awe, touching the hem of his clothes. Father White grabbed him by the shoulders, and suddenly recoiled ten feet or more, like he had received a high voltage shock.

"Are you alright Father?" asked Jack Webster, rushing to his side.

"I've just seen an angel," panted Father White, "s-s-s-sitting on Fine's hat."

"I hate to tell you this," said Jack, through the corner of his mouth, "But there's another one sitting on your shoulder."

# DREAMIN' DREAMS

JUST DAYS AFTER MJ CELEBRATED HIS thirtieth year in America, he was made redundant. A foreman known as the Hound, gripped his hand and said he was sorry to let him go, but the recession had bitten and burst the bubble.

"And I've been with the Hound since '82, you know," MJ says as he tells his story in the bars, "I put out a lot of sweat for that man."

MJ is fifty-something, a small stocky bachelor with big blue eyes and a red porter face. America hasn't made much of an impression on him, fortune-wise or other and he's the same today as the morning he left Ballysollock. Years of work trying to get somewhere and now he realizes there's nowhere to go to. Digging, digging, digging. Day and night. Seven days a week, digging through life in the hope of going back to Ireland with a bundle of money. Now there's no digging and no money. Just time; years of it fell into his lap and he wasn't ready for it.

New-found time is tough to live through, he says. The days are long and he does his best to keep out of harm's way by staying in bed till noon. He relives his life in patches. A silent movie of faded dreams and might-have-beens. There's no blame, just mysteries. He's alone in a one-roomed flat in San Francisco, awake in bed at noon with nothing to fill his day but dreams.

MJ hadn't bargained for this twist of fate and always thought he'd be back living in Ireland long before his working life was over. He had hoped to get enough money together for a small cottage: nothing hectic, with just an acre or two, a few miles outside of some town in the West. Once he had a roof over his head, it would be easy to keep everything else in order. Odd jobs would bring in bread and butter and the dole would buy the beer. That was the plan he came back with after a holiday in Ireland in the Nineties when things were good in America and he had cash. It was his only trip in thirty years. It's hard to go back without having made a fortune; and if you've made it, you don't want to go back.

Every afternoon around three, MJ saunters down Geary Boulevard, regular as a train. Neatly dressed in shirt, slacks and low-grade sneakers, he graciously salutes familiar faces and waves his newspaper at Irish workers in shamrocked vans that hoot as they pass. Some days MJ has a cup of coffee in the Chinese diner in the Mall, it's something to do, a way to pass those extra hours in the day that burden him down like a visiting aunt he can't get rid of. Later he sits on a low brick wall outside the Wells Fargo bank and gently taps the unread newspaper against his knee.

Most days he's joined by Red Carty, a Galway man who came to San Francisco in the Sixties and never went home.

Red hasn't worked in years—he's on the Social Security, sleeps late and drinks early. He's delighted to have company, MJ is new in the hanging-out world and Red subtly shows the way.

Their conversations dance around jigs and reels and ceilli bands from the past. Memories of good times make thirsty talk and soon they move to The '98, a long narrow Irish bar with a red tiled floor and green Formica counter. MJ has to stretch the dollars and returns to his flat after a couple of pints, stopping on the way for a can of beans, bread and eggs, milk and potatoes. He cooks a big feed and falls asleep watching wrestling on television. Next day it's the same routine.

Saturday is the exception. Late-afternoon, Red and MJ meet in the '98 to watch videos of the previous Sunday's sport highlights from Ireland. They keep up with the teams and players, just like they did at home. In many ways they've never left. They're dressed for drinking as if returning from a funeral: MJ in blue suit and white open-neck shirt; Red in porter-brown pants and dark brogues, tweed jacket and cap.

When Red has enough drink supped he talks Irish. A few more down and he cries on MJ's shoulder, sobbing that he left a good farm of land behind when he set sail to make his fortune. Now he has nothing. Nothing here, nothing there. MJ stares gloomily at him and says,

"We'll go back sometime Red."

Red makes contorted, painful faces and shakes his head slowly,

"No MJ," he mumbles, "we'll never go back now, we're gone too long."

By nine or ten o'clock Red has collapsed at the counter and MJ falls into company with long-time immigrants Heart Attack Jack and his brother Milo. When Johnny Foley is tending bar they are allowed sing and Milo opens the evening with "Moonlight in Mayo." Next up: Heart Attack Jack with "Silver Hairs among the Golden." MJ listens in silence, stares at the floor. He's on the town tonight, he's put down another week of unwanted time.

Mrs. Lally and her husband Topper join them around ten-thirty and the smell of perfume and talc reinforces that it is indeed Saturday night. Mrs. Lally corners MJ against the counter and treats him to a monologue on monogamy. Head down, eyes on two dimes on the green Formica, MJ lets it in one ear and out the other. Now she's whispering, coming closer and he feels her hot breath and hears the tobacco wheeze as she rambles on. There's nothing to do but block it out with drink.

After a half-hour, MJ excuses himself to go to the bathroom and when he returns, Mrs. Lally is singing "Nobody's Child" and staring straight at a neon light above the bar that flashes—Budweiser, Budweiser. She's on center stage, thinking she's Evita, getting passionate about being alone in the world. Red snores at the counter, dreaming about milk cans and the cocks of hay he left to rot in the rain. Outside, cop cars scream up and down the street, ambulance sirens waw-waw, waw-waw in the distance. But all the noise and commotion in the world won't wrench Mrs. Lally from her song.

"It's as close as we'll get to home," MJ mutters, counting out money for another round, just to keep the show on the road.

Red wakes before closing time, half-sober, cranky and thirsty. He wants drink and demands entertainment.

"For God's sake," he cries, "it's Saturday night in San Francisco and this place is like a shaggin' morgue."

MJ stares at him, puzzled, as if wondering where he has been until now. Heart Attack Jack and Milo don't need much encouragement and oblige with a duet of "Galway Bay." It's mournful, but not mournful enough for Mrs. Lally, who edges in between them, holds their hands and strangles the song.

A couple of young Paddies playing pool howl at the singers. Red shouts at them to shut up. They shout back. Red knocks over a stool and Johnny Foley the barman, who has suffered enough all night, screams at everyone,

"For the love of Jaysus will ye all shut up! Now!"

The singing and the shouting stop. Red shrugs his shoulders and MJ whispers to hold easy. There's a hush for a few minutes. Glasses clink, pool balls clack. Foley pours himself a large shot of whiskey and slips a tape into the music maker. Barman's revenge, it's the Pogues. The volume is boosted until every glass and bottle in the pub rattle and roll to "Dirty Old Town."

Two verses on, The '98 is singing its head off, dreamin' dreams by the gasworks wall. Heart Attack Jack and Mrs. Lally are dancing. MJ looks puzzled. Young Irish guys and girls are doing a funky waltz around the pool table. Red is whispering,

"We'll never go back, MJ."

"Ah we will," mumbles MJ, "next year, with the help of God. Next year."

He pulls a handful of crumpled dollars from his pocket and calls the barman for two whiskeys and a pack of Camels. Things to pass the time and soothe the soul, while dreamin' dreams about going home.

# Behind Closed Doors

Austin Solan was the youngest dairy manager ever to come to town. A quiet, balding man of thirty-three, he had the slender look of an acetic and it was only a matter of time before he was leading the men's solidarity legion in prayer and good example. Austin and his wife Una had no family. They lived in a stark, one-story manse of grey cut stone that brooded on a small rise at the edge of the town. Once the home of Master McGrath, the Solans bought it for a song, unaware it was a house with a shadow. But on the amount of prayer that Una and Austin packed into a day, nobody thought it necessary to tell them about things supernatural.

One warm Saturday in August while Austin mowed the front lawn, the postman arrived with a letter addressed to the previous owner.

"Why are you bringing this here?" Austin asked quietly, "Don't you know Master McGrath is dead for the last seven years?"

"I'm only doin' my job," apologized the postman, "I know he's dead, an' you know he's dead but the poor woman who wrote the letter don't know that...his sister below in the mental asylum. I was thinkin' it was better to deliver it than to send it back t' her. D' you know what I'm sayin'?"

"You're drunk," Austin said, recoiling from him, "You're drunk and it's only mid-day."

Una shelled peas at the kitchen sink and listened silently to his story.

"God alone knows what letters and parcels that drunk has lost. I should tell the postmaster. That man needs discipline."

He was agitated and walked around the kitchen, fanning his face with the letter.

"And this," he cried, "What are we going to do with...this letter?"

"It's not ours so we shouldn't open it," Una said softly.

"Of course it's not ours. No...but it's just so odd...I mean Master McGrath has been dead for years...and this is from his sister! I mean...what should we do?"

"It's only a letter, Austin," Una smiled, "Don't get so upset about it, it has nothing to do with us."

She took the envelope with the scratchy handwriting from him and left it beside the Child of Prague statue in the hall.

The letter was forgotten about until a few weeks later at breakfast, when she related a dream she'd had the previous night. In the dream, Austin and herself were in the entrance hall of a stately house with black and white checkered marble floors and tall mirrors on the walls. Master McGrath appeared with a whip and chased them through the building until they came to a room which was like their present kitchen, only larger. There were dogs everywhere, barking and frothing at the mouth, they leaped on table and chairs. It was frightening she said, and the next thing she knew, Austin and herself were naked, racing down the town like hares, a pack of wild dogs at their heels and the Master shouting for his letter.

Austin stopped eating.

"Good God! Why did he want the letter?"

Una shook her head.

"I can't remember...the letter only came into it at the end. But his face...I saw it vividly...the purple wart on the side of his nose and all...the big round eyes and the droopy mustache. He shouted that we wronged him."

"Wronged him? The letter? What can be so important about a letter from a deranged sister?"

It wasn't what he said but how he said it. Una shivered and goose pimples tingled the back of her neck. She sensed a strange feeling sneak into the kitchen.

"Austin," she said shakily, "we better say a prayer, quickly."

There and then they crossed themselves, bowed their heads and recited a decade of the Rosary.

After work that evening, as he approached the gravel avenue to his home, Austin saw a man in black walking away from the front door. He wondered who could it be, as the figure crossed the lawn and disappeared over the fence. Father Hannon? But why hop the fence rather than come down the drive? Couldn't be Father Hannon. Must be someone else.

Una said she had no no callers and when Austin insisted he saw a man leave, she stood still in the middle of the kitchen and said quietly,

"Austin, surely you don't think I'm hiding something from you?"

"No. No, it's just that I'm sure I saw a man leave this house. That's all."

They didn't speak for the rest of the evening and Una went to bed early and prayed herself to sleep. That night she dreamed about a man prowling outside the house; he was young and good looking and she saw him come to the kitchen window, beckoning her. She opened the window and he reached in and fondled her breasts until Master McGrath came running across the lawn with a gun in his hand. Una woke sweating. Austin lay beside her, snoring erratically.

Next morning at breakfast, they ate in silence until Una left the letter beside her husband and said,

"You might drop that off at the post-office today if you get a chance."

He nodded and slipped the envelope into his jacket pocket. He would write across it in red pen, *Return To Sender, Addressee Deceased*. That would do it, he reasoned.

Torrential rain slowed Austin's driving to a crawl. The car roof rattled with pellets of fury and wipers slish-sloshed waves of water across the windscreen, blurring the world. But he didn't notice the downpour so much, Austin was wondering if the heat from the letter next to his heart was real or imaginary. Troubling himself into a trance, he nosed the car deeper down the flooded road until the engine choked in the hollow outside the Market House. Muddy water oozed into the vehicle and Austin abandoned it and waded the rest of the way to work.

Drenched and preoccupied he trudged into his office where Terry Morris, his assistant manager, waited with a worried look. Dairy Crisis: the butter was not balling and the butter-makers were alarmed.

"My God!" Austin muttered, pulling a white lab coat over his soggy clothes.

Batty Gill, the head butter-maker, was baffled. In all his years by the churn he had never failed to transform cream into butter before. He followed Austin and Terry around the plant while they took readings and frowned into vats. After tastes, samples and stringent testing, the bossmen concluded that everything was in accordance with the book. There was no reason why the butter should not ball. Batty was encouraged to keep churning. Austin suggested that it may just be some freak humidity caused by the downpour. The butter-maker rubbed his jaw and said that whatever the reason, it was certainly something beyond his control.

When the dairy gold failed to form by lunch time, the normally noisy canteen was silent. Austin couldn't eat with worry. Some old hands whispered that this was only a sign of something more serious afoot. Matta Kelly, a milk strainer, hinted that buttermaking had been taken for granted ever since the churn moved from the cottage to the state dairy. He said that just as the head of the household had to accept responsibility for butter-making in the old days, the dairy manager had to carry the can in these times.

That afternoon, word of the butter crisis had rippled down town and Father Hannon telephoned Austin and pledged his prayers. He suggested blessing the churns if things didn't improve by evening. But Austin played it down, explained that the problem was due to freak weather conditions.

"Still, a drop of Holy Water never did any harm," Father Hannon reminded, "especially in a superstitious part of the country like here."

With no butter to show, Terry Morris brought Austin home early that evening. Una was scrubbing carrots at the kitchen sink, yellow rubber gloves stretched to her elbows. She jolted when she saw him. He was exhausted, drenched with worry and rain.

"What happened?" Una asked.

"Bad day. Bad day. The butter wouldn't ball."

His voice croaked and she tensed and whispered,

"Sit down Austin, I'll make you a cup of tea."

She left the day's mail before him and then he remembered Master McGrath's letter was still in his jacket pocket. He hopped from the chair and uttered what sounded like a squawk. Una asked if he was alright, but he didn't hear her, he was staring at the soggy letter whose ink had run through his clothes from head to toes. Austin could feel the cold thin ink all over his wet body, the words of Master McGrath's sister seeping into his skin like tattoos. He felt tactile hallucinations, and slapped legs and arms where they began to tingle. Una thought he was having a fit or seizure and stammered,

"Are you alright Austin?"

He flapped about saying,

"I must have a bath, must have a bath."

Austin dashed to the bathroom and she heard water cascade into the tub. Steam rose from the letter on the table and nervously Una picked it up with a spatula and tossed it into the coal burning stove. Muttering a Hail Mary, she retreated to the sink, expecting something to happen, some sort of explosion or inexplicable event, something supernatural. Nothing. From down the corridor came the sound of water thundering into the bath. A tap winced and then there was silence.

"My God," she muttered, "I should make a hot drink for Austin."

Una knocked politely on the bathroom door before entering.

"This will do you good," she said, halting abruptly when she noticed the tub was empty.

"Austin? Austin?" she called curiously, looking around the bathroom. She heard a rustle overhead and saw a big black raven perched on the shower rail. Feathers dripping, eyes darting with distress, the bird began to flap its wings hysterically.

"Austin!" she screamed, banging the door shut, "Austin! There's a crow in the loo!"

She searched the house but there was no trace of Austin. The raven flapped around the bathroom, squawking and croaking. It didn't make sense. Austin couldn't have disappeared, he wouldn't put a toe outside the door without telling her, he wouldn't even go to the toilet without letting her know. She wandered aimlessly around the kitchen, then eased into a chair and prayed.

Half-way through the Lord's Prayer, it struck her that Austin was overcome by the butter crisis and had returned to the creamery. Then the bird somehow got into the bathroom. That was it, she thought and gave God thanks for the insight.

When Austin wasn't home by midnight, she began to panic and called the dairy. Nobody there, so she called Terry Morris and interrupted his lovemaking. He hadn't seen Austin since driving him home that evening and news of his superior's disappearance jolted him. He volunteered to come over to the house, but Una said that wasn't necessary, that there was probably some simple explanation. Maybe he had gone to see Father Hannon.

"But it's a terrible night out," Terry said, "and he has no car."

Waiting for her husband, Una had a fitful night. Awake at dawn, she felt the bed for Austin and shivered at his empty place. She rushed to the phone and called Father Hannon. He came over immediately.

"It's bizarre," the priest muttered when he heard her story, "bizarre."

"Would it have anything to do with the butter crisis?" she asked hesitantly.

He rocked uncomfortably in his chair and said,

"It's a coincidence, just a coincidence."

That was the feedback he was getting. Coincidences that are somehow connected occur: like the blood red moon that rose on the night the Viet Nam war ended. He had seen it with his own eyes. And his heart missed a beat when he remembered the morning the horse burst into Hannifin's Bar, hours before one of the sons was killed by a run-away Ford Mustang in California.

"I think," he said, slowly rising from the chair, "we should notify the police about Austin's disappearance. I don't want to alarm you but it may be serious."

The police took a long statement from Una, Father Hannon at her side, stone faced. When Sergeant Malone asked questions about her husband's habits, worries and hurries, the priest reminded him that Austin was a saint. Sergeant Malone nodded and closed his blue notebook with a sympathetic sigh.

"We'll file a missing person's report immediately," he said.

Rattled by Austin's disappearance, Una didn't think to tell either priest or police about the crow in the bathroom. But in light of the crisis, the bird didn't matter and all day she used the toilet by the kitchen rather than deal with it. The phone rang intermittently, friends pledging support, parents weeping, neighbours sniffing. And everyone heard the same story: Austin left the kitchen to have a bath and disappeared.

That evening, around the time her husband usually returned home, the door bell chimed and she rushed from the kitchen. The man in black was a stranger and for a moment she thought it was a young priest. He was in his mid-twenties maybe, and had a small leather holdall over his shoulder.

"Yes?" Una said.

"I've come to catch the crow," he announced with a shy smile.

"It's in the bathroom," she said nervously.

Una stood in the hall while he captured the bird, talking to it, coaxing it, cawing to it. He reappeared from the washroom, proudly displaying his squirming hold-all.

"It won't bother you again," he said.

Una muttered thanks and he walked away with the bird in his bag. Later that night when she cleaned the bathroom of feathers and droppings, it struck her that he was a replica of the young man who fondled her breasts in the dream.

Austin Solan never returned to his wife. He seemed to have fallen off the face of the earth. Police couldn't find him. Psychics couldn't dowse him, priests failed to pray him back home. Una grieved. Shunned friends and neighbours. Rarely went out and invited nobody to her home. Every other week the young man in black came to see her and they sat in the kitchen for hours, barely speaking, always sensing. His name was Johnny and as time wore on she learned his likes and dislikes. One spoon of sugar in tea, lots of butter with potatoes. On a cold evening when he remarked that he loved flannel sheets like they had in the old days, she said,

"That's what I've on the bed tonight."

Every Saturday evening for years after, Batty Gill the butter-maker and Matta Kelly watched Una wander from shop to shop while they drank their weekend pints in Bridgey Looney's bar.

"And she still thinks poor Austin Solan will come back some day," Bridgey would sadly say.

"He won't be back," Matta would sigh, "that man went with the river. Suicide. He'll never be heard of again."

Bridgey moaned that great credit was due to Una for staying in the town, but of course the woman was unhinged by it all. Imagine, she told the men, after all these years, poor Mrs. Solan still bought socks and underwear for her vanished husband and shopped for two when she went to the grocery shop and the butcher. Even got him cowboy books from the library.

"A tragedy," Batty usually said, "that's the only explanation for it."

"But it had to happen sometime," Matta would insist, glass empty, waiting for a refill, "Sure that house is haunted."

Bridgey would nod and fill two pints for the old timers. For the umpteenth time she heard the horrific story of Johnny Doyle, the bird catcher who fell in love with Lucinda McGrath, the Master's sister. Johnny had a vociferous appetite and could not see enough of his love. And when the Master stumbled on them coupling in the bathroom one evening, he lost his senses and shot the bird catcher through the head with a pistol from the revolution. Lucinda went crazy and the Master was acquitted on self-defense.

"That house is haunted," Matta said, "sure it couldn't be otherwise. The place would give you shivers to look at it. You'd go mad living in that house."

Up in the manse, saucepans boiled over on the stove and the Glenn Miller Band blared from the radio. In her Saturday night kitchen, Una was oblivious to the world, as she danced the Chatanooga Cho-cho with Johnny Doyle the bird catcher.

# JACKASS BLUES

DURING THAT DARK, SLOW PERIOD BETWEEN
New Year and Lent, a black ass sauntered into
town. Sleek as a seal, it had the fine features of a
thoroughbred and moved gracefully through the
street with a confidence that its working class
brethren lack. It seemed curious about the town
and gazed at the old wooden shop-fronts like
tourists did, peered into laneways and stared at
posters and notices tacked to telegraph poles.
The animal showed no interest in people and
nobody bothered it, thinking it was a stray just
passing through.

After a few days, it discovered the televisions
in the window of Harney's Electrical Emporium
and would stand in the footpath watching Sesame
Street, Bosco or whatever programmes were showing.
When Bruce Harney switched off the sets, the ass
would move on to spend the night in the shadows
of a back lane. Then one evening when Harney
pulled the plug, the animal got indignant and

thumped its head against the shop window a few times. Bruce roared at him to 'bum off' and the animal lashed his hind legs against the window. The smash of glass brought everyone outside and the black ass galloped around the town square, bucking like a rodeo star.

Harney went to the police to make a statement for insurance purposes and Sergeant Malone determined that the donkey should be impounded. Next morning he gathered a posse of local animal handlers: Coyne the butcher, Coco Ryan the blacksmith, Murt Lyons, Gimp McDonagh and Fonsie Duggan the horse-blocker. The butcher brought along a gun 'just in case'. He took control of the gang, psyching up the handlers until they were as rabid as a lynch mob.

"Chase him up Boland's Lane," he ordered, "then we can lasso him. But we want to do it now. Immediately. Or else that animal will maul someone."

The posse stalked the black ass for days but he outsmarted them every time, becoming a hero with street urchins and local dead-beats. As if aware of the sanctuary afforded to outlaws of old, the animal now took refuge in the church grounds at night. Father White would see him shelter under the trees, hear him urinate by the side of the house. Even with the gates locked and chained, the animal still somehow entered and Father White felt besieged by evil, his holy space violated. He urged the donkey hunters to double their efforts and hinted that the butcher's gun might be their only solution.

Before the week passed, the donkey gained a few supporters who protested against the posse. Receiving no quarter from Sergeant Malone, they came to Father White with their pleas. First came Gretta Green, the madwoman from Frowhell. She pleaded with the priest to call off the posse, explaining that asses were God's favorite animal and should be free to roam and do whatever they wanted. Coming closer she whispered,

"For all you know that ass could be here on a mission."

Standing in pouring rain, Gretta referred to the bible and listed countless roles the species had played, reminding the priest of the many tight spots where asses had come to God's rescue. Father White nodded, rubbed his tired eyes; he set her mind at rest with a prayer that God would deliver the ass to safety as in the past.

A few hours later he had a second caller: MJ Kelly, another ass lover, who extolled the animal's beauty and grace and pleaded that Greenpeace, Dúchas or the R.S.P.C.A. be notified about its presence. MJ said it was a rare ass and that it might have escaped from some zoo, like the one the Englishman had in County Wicklow.

Vera Cruise the bank manager's wife arrived under a yellow golfer's umbrella that said Pernod. She grabbed the priest by the hand and he could feel her bones shivering when she whispered,

"There's a soul trapped inside that ass. Look at his eyes, they're the eyes of a man in pain. A martyr. You have to bless that animal Father. Say prayers over him."

He looked at her with compassion and said,

"Vera, you've been drinking again and it doesn't suit you."


Father White had terrible dreams that night: armed with a bucket of Holy Water and a shaker, he was dueling with the ass in the town square; people hung out windows to follow the action. The parishioners were pitting him against a demon, putting him in a spot, making him earn his keep. Then the town became Jerricho and Father White saw Jesus and the apostles, all riding jet black donkeys. The holymen carried huge guns and the donkeys grew wings and turned into firey dragons. He was no match for them and lifted a manhole cover and descended underground for safety.

Next morning the priest was praying, sitting on the edge of his bed when he heard an urgent knock on the door. More trouble, he thought, wrapping a brown dressing gown around himself and trundling downstairs.

The man at the door was Trick Rodgers, an animal jobber from the far end of the parish.

"I'll catch that ass," he said bluntly, "but I'll have to be paid first. If I fail, you'll get the money back."

A fee of five pounds was quickly agreed and before the jobber changed his mind, Father White hurried and took five crinkled notes from the church coffers. He looked Trick in both eyes and said,

"Have that animal out of town by tomorrow. I don't care how you do it, just get him out of here."

Trick tipped his hat and said quietly,

"God's will will be done."


When the the daily communicants dribbled to Mass next morning, the ass was lying on his side at Cassidy's Corner. It was the talk of the church, especially when Father White offered up thanks to God for delivering the town from evil. Trick was loading the beast on a hay cart when the Mass-goers poured from the church. A crowd gathered around to get a close view.

"That's a hungry ass," said Tim Wynn, "Hah? But look at the head o' teeth he has. Hah?"

"What age d'you think he's Trick?" shouted Paddy Hynes.

"Old enough to have sense," muttered the jobber, rising a laugh from the onlookers that unsettled the bound animal. Women screamed when he threshed his legs and Trick shouted,

"Stand back or he'll ate ye!"

The loaded cart creaked out of town at funeral pace. Father White watched from behind the lace curtained windows of his breakfast room and said,

"Thanks God. Thanks."

The donkey recovered in a stone-walled field behind Rodger's house, where he had great forests of thistles and a fine view of the Atlantic. Trick broadcast that the animal was at stud but when a few clients brought their mares, the jack ignored them and pranced around playing hard to get. Rumors spread about his virility and soon he was left alone to rest his chin on the stone wall of his lodgings and look out at the ocean. Eventually Trick forgot about him, left him in the field like an abandoned car.

Time passed slowly, spring was wet and windy and the jobber spent most of his time in pubs. When summer arrived, the sun didn't shine often and one grey day when Trick was cycling to town, the postman flagged him down. He looked at him blankly and said,

"Trick? Do you know the Frenchman an' his wife that bought Paddy Keogh's place beyond in Carageen?"

"The two hippies?"

"That's them...well they asked if I knew of anyone who had a good ass for sale. I told 'em I'd say it to you."

"They want a good ass?"

"As good as they'll get, I s'pose."

"I've an ass," said Trick offering the postman a cigarette,

"a right good ass. I don't have any use for him and it's a pity. Maybe he'd suit them."

"Sure he'd suit 'em grand Trick...an' they wouldn't be workin' him too hard...I'll tell 'em that when I'm over that way again."

"The best thing to do so," said Trick, "is for me to write 'em a letter and give it to you."

Trick got a pencil from the postman and scribbled a note on the back of a cigarette box.

*I have a good ass for sale. Strong as a horse. Price £10. T. Rodgers, Tobbarnave.*

Sitting in the front seat of a yellow Renault van, the postman directed the buyers to Trick's farm. Bouncing over pot-holed roads, the strangers smiled at each other, shook their heads at the beauty of the heathery land and the quaintness of its people. Trick heard the motor approaching and was at the gate to welcome them. They introduced themselves, smoked a round of hand-rolled cigarettes and then the jobber brought them to the donkey. Starved of company, he trotted to his visitors like a puppy.

"A fine animal, God knows. And a strong animal Trick," praised the postman.

"That ass is as strong as any horse and aisier to manage and feed," the jobber announced.

"Ten pounds you say?" the Frenchman said.

"Ten Irish pounds. And I'd get twice that if I advertised him in the paper."

The couple smiled, nodded and rattled to each other in French. The ass stood by the other side of the wall, listening to his fate dealers. There was talk of a cart, harness and tackle and when the ass raised his head to protest, the bargain was struck.

That night while the ass slept, Trick slipped a noose around his neck and in the morning brought him to the French people. He waved the animal good-bye with the sincerity of a mother sending her son to boarding school. The ass brayed but Trick walked away without looking back.

Returning home from the cattle mart in Ballyhobbit almost a week later, Trick went into Aggie Ryan's for a drink. Aggie did most of the talking, Trick not paying much heed until she said,

"God wasn't that awful about the poor French people below in Paddy Keogh's place. Very sad. Awful sad sure..."

"Who's that Aggie?" he asked.

"Ah you know 'em. A big tall fella with whiskers an' a black tam an' a lady—I don't know if she's his wife or not—she has long straggly hair and she wears long skirts an' big hob nail boots."

"I know 'em." said Trick, "Nice people. Hippies. What happened to them?"

"It seems they bought an ass from someone...an' whether he was broken or not, I don't know...but he attacked them."

"Jesus-Mary-and-Joseph!" Trick blurted, stuffed a cigarette into his mouth. "What happened Aggie? They were attacked by an ass?"

"Well I'm not so sure what happened. Tommy Reilly was here today and he said the hippies were tacklin' the ass when he turned on them...he bolted from the stable an' kicked the door shut on 'em as he went out. They were locked in the stable for three days and three nights, tryin' to get out an' couldn't. If Margo Flynn hadn't come along an' heard 'em roarin' they'd have starved to death. They'd be there yet. That's an awful lonesome place they live in down there. Sweet Heart of Jesus but didn't wan of the Keogh boys hang 'em selves in that same stable?"

"He did. But were the French people...hurt? Did the ass...bite 'em or anything?" asked Trick, shifting in his seat.

"Sure they were in a terrible way after it. Shocked more than anything, accordin' to Tommy."

"Well as long as they weren't hurt or bitten, that's the main thing. An ass is a hard animal to handle. People think they're foolish, but they're not. Not by a long shot."

"Oh sure they were lucky. That ass could have ate 'em, Tommy said."

Up town in Egan's bar, Trick heard the ass had pitched Pat Hamil from his bicycle over in Clochar. The animal knocked walls all the way from Carageen to Cohey, letting hundreds of stock roam from home.

"That ass is on the rampage," said Sonny Cullen, a heavy whiskey drinker. He shook his head, glanced at Trick and warned, "Jesus Christ Trick, when he gets as far as you, you'd better have an elephant gun."

"An' Trick, if you don't mind me sayin' so," wheezed Peter Egan the publican, "but you shouldn't have dumped that ass so near home. An' especially to them two poor hippies. Sure great God almighty, the nearest they ever got to an ass was on the television. You should have kept that beauty for the Fair of Spancill Hill and sold him to some wan above in Kildare or Meath, where he could graze lawns. But...Excuse me gentlemen."

He broke off: Mrs. Egan was calling from the kitchen. He returned a few minutes later and whispered to Trick,

"Herself said that Sergeant Malone is lookin' for you. He was up at Aggie's. If you want...you can slip out through the kitchen and down the yard to the backlane."

Trick nodded slightly, took a sip from his drink and nipped into the kitchen. The jobber's glass was in the sink when the lawman jabbed his head into the bar.

"God bless ye men," he saluted, looking around, "Anyone see the jobber Rodgers?"

"He was here earlier Sergeant," wheezed Peter, "he might be up in Aggie's. He was in town alright."

"Who?" crooned Sonny Cullen, putting his hand behind his ear.

"You know him Sonny," said the sergeant, "Trick Rodgers the cattle jobber. The tubby fella with the white coat and green hat."

"Oh yes, yes, yes. Yes of course," said Sonny, turning towards the sergeant, "you might find him in Lala Vaughan's. He goes there sometimes. If I'm not mistaken but Lala is some relation of his."

"Alright, thanks men," muttered Malone and left.

"Whether the law or d'ass gets to him first," sighed Sonny, "but I'm thinkin' Trick is in the shit."

Trick hid at home for two days, sleeping in the loft and peering from the skylight every time he heard a sound. The postman banged on the door one evening but got no response. Talking to himself, he walked around the house, rattled windows, asked the hens who was feeding them and left again. Then it was quiet for what seemed eternity.

Heavy pounding on the front door spun Trick from a shallow sleep. The Law. He crawled out of bed and listened to Malone and Constable Collins walk around the house, commenting on the state of the place.

"His bike is here," Collins said and they banged on the back door and rapped the windows.

"Rodgers! Get up and open the door," called Sergeant Malone, "We know you're at home."

More pounding and thumping, threats of bursting down the door; talk of a warrant.

"Hello!" cried Trick suddenly, sticking his head out the skylight, "Hello. Who's that?"

"Police!" shouted the young cop, "Open up!"

The jobber met them in his vest and trousers, braces looped at the knees.

"Mr. Rodgers," the sergeant announced, "we want you to come down to the station with us."

"Station?" echoed Trick.

"The barracks!" barked the constable.

"Are you comin' or do we have to arrest you?" asked Malone, inflating his chest and poising his head like a cobra.

"Arrest me?" cried Trick, pulling up his braces, "What in the name of Christ are ye arresting me for?"

Malone took a black book from his tunic pocket and read some mumbo-jumbo about rights, but Trick wasn't really listening. He was looking over the sergeant's shoulder at a black ass cantering down the road.

"That's grand," said Trick, "That's grand. I understand all that...but what I want to know is what are ye arresting me for?"

"For sellin' an animal that wasn't yours to sell," replied the young policeman. "The ass that Father White paid you to catch wasn't your's to sell and you sold him to a couple of foreigners who wouldn't know an ass from a giraffe— thereby endangering their lives and the lives of the public in general."

"You're wrong," protested Trick. "That ass you're talkin' about and the ass I sold to them French people are two different asses. That ass behind you is the ass I caught for the priest."

The black ass was galloping hard towards the house, his jaws hinged like an open scissors. The policemen scattered around the shack, skidding on chicken shit and discarded tea leaves. The donkey hawed like a fog horn, Malone shouted,

" Rodgers—call off that animal!"

"Hold aisey!" roared Trick and to his astonishment, the donkey shuddered to a stop and turned docile as a lamb.

"That's a good boy," muttered the jobber with relief, "that's a good fella. Hold aisey now. These nice men won't harm you. Hold aisey now."

Malone peeped around the gable of the house and made a dash for the patrol car, followed by his constable. Safely in the car he rolled down the window and shouted,

"Rodgers! You haven't heard the end of this!"

Trick put his hands on his hips, looked at the ass and said,

"What in the name of Jaysus are you doin' here, you black bastard. Don't you know that I get into enough shit without the likes of you rakin' it for me? Jaysus Christ Almighty, couldn't you have been nice to them two poor hippies above in Carageen and have a soft live an' a bed to lie 'n at night. Why in the name of Christ did you act the bollix an' shit on us all?"

The ass raised his head and swaggered a few steps closer. He stared at Trick with deep black eyes. This is no ass, Trick was forced to think as he felt the animal harangue him. He sprang back into the kitchen when he thought he heard a bass voice say,

"I'm not just an ass, you know."

"Fuck off outta here!" ordered Trick, standing behind the door.

"Hey listen," he was hearing, "it's okay Trick. I can explain..."

"Shag off!" roared Rodgers, bolting the door, "The butcher was right. The gun! The gun and a High Mass. An' I'll pay for the Mass. The devil! That's what you are!"

"Trick?" came a voice from under the door.

"Don't call me Trick you prick!"

"Well then, Mr. Rodgers...look...I know this is very strange ...and it's not everyone I can connect with, but if you can give me a few minutes of your time I can explain everything..."

"Don't explain anything...that's my job. Just shag off out of here!"

A couple of seconds later hooves cannonaded the door and Trick swore and cursed and invoked all the gods and angels, saints and sages he had ever heard of, to rid him of the affliction. He sweated and his throat dried up asking for forgiveness for misdeeds and bad deals. The battering got louder and the kitchen vibrated like the belly of a drum. Dishes shivered and pots rattled until Trick thought the four walls would collapse around him. When an old jam jug crashed from the dresser, Trick lashed a running kick that hit the door as the ass's hooves touched the wood. He rattled the animal to his teeth.

"Up yours too," snarled the voice outside, withdrawing to the shelter of the cart house.

Trick sat at the table and smoked a cigarette. It was a day of shocks: visits from the law and talking asses, a dealer's doomsday. Attacked on all fronts, he sighed, looking at his mother's jug shattered on the flag floor. He had another cigarette and glanced out the window: it would rain again soon. That's the type of day it is, he sighed and decided to put down a fire.

He busied himself around the house and it occurred to him that if he was anywhere else in the world, this cloud might have a silver lining. A talking animal would be a valuable piece of property in America. When he worked in Chicago there used be a television program starring a talking horse. Though getting this ass to America would be complicated and probably backfire. The television station in Dublin wouldn't be able to handle the idea. A circus might be my best bet, thought Trick. A voice announced under the door,

"We've company."

A few vehicles were parked out at the road. Trick recognised the hippies' yellow motorvan, the butcher's truck and the patrol car. More cars drew up, doors slammed and a crowd swelled outside the gate. A bull horn squelched and blared:

"Rodgers? Rodgers can you hear me? This is Sergeant Malone. Step out of your house."

"Stay put," said the bass voice, "I'll cover you."

"Rodgers!" the sergeant again called, "Come out. We know you're at home, you have the fire down."

Trick stuck his head out the door.

"What ails ye?" he shouted.

The bull horn screeched.

"We want you to help us in our inquiries," Sergeant Malone hailed across two acres of rain.

Trick assessed the situation and pulled on a white cattle coat and trilby hat, grabbed a cudgel and stepped outside. He closed the door, muttering to the ass,

"Any jig acting now my friend and we are both down the sink."

"No problem. Just act as if everything is normal. I'm cool."

The jobber took his time crossing the field and his reception party were dripping wet when he reached them.

"I'm glad ye came," he muttered to Malone, "because I want to see the priest right quick."

"Why? Is it confessions you want?"

"Look, bring me down to Father White and tell the rest of these people to shag off home out of the rain because they couldn't be in a more dangerous place than here at this time. Didn't you hear about the devil appearin' at the dancehall above in Galway and the havoc that he caused?"

"What are you on about?" asked Malone, getting annoyed, "What has the devil to do with this, except that you're the fuckin' devil. Are you goin' to sprout hooves and horns for us?"

"Do you see that black ass?" Trick sighed, "Well that's no ass, I'll have you know. That's the devil."

Trick's words surprised Malone.

"The devil?" he muttered, turning his eyes on the ass, "No ....You're ravin'...you're dotin'...no, that's just a mad ass."

"Look, that's the devil and I know it. What's more, he spoke to me, and write that down in your book if you like and I'll stand by it."

Blue lights flashing, the patrol car hurried to the parochial house and Trick was ushered to the sitting-room while the priest finished his dinner and listened to the sergeant's report. Father White was pale and harrowed when he came into the sitting room, sucking his teeth.

"How're you feeling Mr. Rodgers?" he cautiously asked, dropping into an armchair.

"How would you feel if you met the devil?"

The priest inhaled very deeply and joined hands over his lap.

"The devil?" he sighed like a falling bomb.

"That's right."

"Let me tell you first Mr. Rodgers that the evil spirit can manifest itself in many forms and we are most vulnerable when we are fatigued, as often happens in certain kinds of weather. Why, I knew a man one time who was convinced the devil was always hovering around before a thunderstorm burst...just like today's weather...heavy, wet and clammy," he smiled weakly and shook his head, "It may be nothing more than your nerves Mr. Rodgers..."

"Excuse me one second, Father, but what about the time the devil appeared in the dancehall above in Galway? Didn't you tell the story yourself from the pulpit below in the church? I'm only doin' my duty as a good Christian, reportin' what I know. There's no harm in that, and I thought that any priest, high or low would only be too delighted to have the chance to go to bat with the devil. T'would be good for promotion and good for the parish too. And furthermore," said Trick leaning towards him, "but t'is yourself that's the cause of all this trouble and I'll have to tell the newspapers and the bishop if there's any damage done."

"For God sake will you stop it," snapped Father White, rising from his chair. He turned away from Trick to blow his nose and wipe his forehead. "Look," he continued, "don't tell me that what started out a wild jackass hanging around the town has...has...has now become the devil and talks to you."

"I will," said Trick, "and what's more...I don't want him hanging above around my house because I'm not smart enough to talk to him all day, so I'm here to tell you that I'm bringing him back down here and you can put him out there in the orchard and ask him riddles."

Father White closed his eyes and Trick thought he was praying. After a while he took a pack of cigarettes from his pocket and offered one to the jobber. He said softly,

"If you don't mind me sayin' so, but I think you are taking this donkey business too seriously. Hmm? You know, the situation with the French people and all that... I know you were doing us a favor by catching the animal...and things didn't go well for you...I know that people here believe in the old superstitions as well and you see, it might be only natural...that you might think there is some...well...evil influence involved."

"Oh?" said Trick, stirring in his chair.

"Yes. It can be a common enough thing...by the way would you care for a little drop of brandy? It will help you relax."

"I wouldn't mind, to tell you the truth."

They clinked glasses in good health and the priest passed an hour or so telling stories about the supernatural and solving mysteries with the wave of his hand. When the jobber pressed him again about the Galway dancehall incident he topped up the tumblers and said,

"Mr. Rodgers...you know...forget about Galway for a while ...I think I should call Sergeant Malone and see if we can straighten out this affair...after all, you were only was trying to rid us of a nuisance."

"Sure I walked right into it again," said Trick and the priest excused himself from the room.

Everything was smoothed over in a couple of minutes. Another donkey would be found for the French people if Trick would promise to keep the black ass on his own farm. The priest smiled and the jobber said,

"Maybe you're right Father, sure maybe I was only hearing things."

"Well I didn't say that...what I meant was..."

"I know, I know...sure it might be all over when I go home."

"More than likely. But you did the right thing by coming to me."

The telephone jingled impatiently in another room.

"I hope it's not bad news," Father White muttered with a frown.

The priest had a puzzled smile when he returned a couple of seconds later,

"It's for you Mr. Rodgers," he said.

"Me? Wanted on the telephone? Who? Where is it?"

"Out the door and the first room on your left," directed the priest, "the phone is on my desk in the study."

Trick picked up the receiver and said,

"Hello?"

"Trick?"

"Yes, this is me. Who's this?"

"It's me. Look, I'm calling from the phone box down at Carey's Cross. I rang the barracks and they said you were with the padre..."

"Hello? Hello! Who 'm I talkin' to?"

"This is Hee-Haw. Trick...look, I was just calling to ask you to leave the padre out of this. You know, no heavy prayers, Holy Water, Benediction or that sort of jazz?"

"All that'll be sound," said Trick quietly. If he was anywhere other than the parochial house, he'd blaze the caller from the wire with a volley of abuse.

"So how's it going down there with you? Alright I hope."

"Very well entirely. And with yourself?"

"Okey-dokey. The cop car passed over a couple of times and slowed down for a look. But no trauma."

"I see. Well that's good."

"Yeah. Yeah, and the postman called. Had no mail for you. Footless of course."

The operator came on the line—

"Hello? Hello, Bunowan Two? Insert four pence please."

Both parties ignore him.

"And it look's like the rain will clear up after a while," said the caller.

"Great. Well thank's for callin'. I better get back to Father White."

"Okay Trick. Take it slowly. Over and out."

The receiver dropped and clunked against the walls of the telephone kiosk. Trick heard the caller awkwardly leave the box and clip-clop down the road. He looked up at a statue of Jesus standing on the priest's mantelpiece and asked,

"Why me Lord? Why me?"

And without opening His mouth the Lord answered,

"Trick, these things are sent to try us. Relax."

# Song for Angie

SUNNY SLEPT WITH HER MOUTH OPEN, ONE arm over the bed clothes. Her hair was short, bleached blonde and her face was pale and oval shaped. High on her arm peeped a cheap tattoo of a small blue star. Over the bed hung a poster of John Lennon and on the floor her clothes sat where she undressed the night before. The phone rang and she stirred, pulled the covers over her head and let it ring. Awake, eyes closed, she waited for the answer machine to click in, but the caller hung up without leaving a message.

She lay still. Her mouth was parched and she wondered what time it was. On the sidewalk outside, somebody tinkered with a car engine: wrenches clinked, metal winced. A tape of Mexican music played across the street. She heard empty beer cans being crushed underfoot, more cans popping open. Probably early afternoon. Saturday in San Francisco.

Sunny pieced together the previous night. She'd played a gig at the Brown Cow on Polk Street, just herself and her guitar. While she thought about the show, the phone rang again. The answer machine clicked in and when she heard her mother's nervous voice calling from Ireland, she tumbled out of bed and grabbed the receiver.

"Mama..."

"Is that you Sunny?" echoed the words in trans-Atlantic static.

"Yeah. How are you?"

"Not too good, love. I'm afraid we have a bit of bad news for you. Aunty Angie is dead."

"Oh Jesus."

Telephone clamped between head and shoulder, Sunny searched for cigarettes, while her mother broke the news from Ireland: Angie had taken her own life.

"Christ," whispered Sunny, "I can't believe it."

"We can't either, love. The whole parish is in a terrible way about it. Timothy found her in the cow house."

The news shattered Sunny and after the call, she sat on a floor cushion and had another cigarette. Angie hung herself. She frowned at her purple finger nails, replaying her mother's news. Timothy found her in the cow house. Your father was talking to her an hour or so before and she was in great form. The poor soul left a note for Father White. It'll be read at the inquest.

Images of the cow shed floated into Sunny's mind and she saw Timothy, standing in the dung splattered yard, wearing a brown coat and cap, Wellington boots with tops turned down. Timothy, that bird of a man with the drooling nose, who eternally wandered in and out of the house, searching for something, oblivious to everything. Oblivious to Angie until he found her hanging in the cow shed. She smelled the dampness and the dung, heard the emptiness and saw the toes of her aunt's brogues swaying ever so slightly in the gloomy shed.

It was a day for wearing black. Black jeans, t-shirt and black leather jacket...How could Angie do it? How could she get a rope, make the knot, climb up and hang herself from a beam in the cow shed? Sunny sat on the bed and pulled on her boots. Zipped up her leather jacket and grabbed sunglasses from the top of the refrigerator.

Two steps at a time she clattered down the stairs, rattling the house to hell. Out the door and into the sunlight, she turned left without looking and went down 20th Street. Haunted by an out-of-tune piano, she turned into Harrison and walked along the bright side of the street, heading for nowhere in particular. It was as quiet as an Irish village in the evening sun. Not another soul on the street but her.

A few blocks later, at the corner of Lime and Harrison she stopped to get her bearings, plot a course. Then she noticed Jonah's Bark, a shanty bar wedged between two carpet outlets. Something drew her to the pub.

Once inside, she remembered having been there before. You couldn't forget the decor. It was fitted out like the deck of an old sailing ship: masts, tarry ropes, brass rimmed portholes. Stuffed gulls of every description perched in the most unlikely places—the bathrooms, telephone box, bar stools. She'd found this place one Saturday when Borg and herself were tripping. Strange. Someone said it was once a waterfront bar, but was moved inland—lock, stock and barrel when the bay-view rents soared.

A few solitary drinkers hunched along the counter, staring silently at the barman who fed tropical fish in a huge tank behind the bar. A skittle-shaped giant with a shaved head and a white apron, he said in a shrill voice,

"I'll be right with you, honey,"

Sunny settled herself on a stool, left sunglasses on the counter and lit a cigarette. She wanted a pint of Guinness, but he didn't have any, so she settled for cider. Like the others, she drank in silence and watched the feeding fish. She crossed her knees, left foot swinging nervously. Angie, above all people. What went wrong? Was there nobody she could have turned to?

Sunny hadn't been in touch with Angie for almost six months. That was when her aunt called from Ireland to announce she'd got the telephone installed. Sunny never followed up with the promised call, and that was the last contact they'd had. Now she was gone. A hole in space. Sweet Jesus.

For years they had been like mother and daughter. Growing up, Sunny spent more time in her aunt's house that at home. Angie's house was peaceful, there were no brawling brothers or wailing wains, no moaning mother or phantom father. Angie's place was calm and warm, a blessed place of refuge.

Sunny drank in long draughts and called for another pint of cider as she was coming to the end of her glass. She took a break from thinking and looked at the fish in the tank, following a blue-tailed bullet until she drifted back to Angie's kitchen. It was here she did her school homework on a green covered card table that had belonged to Timothy's mother. When the learning was finished, she ran errands for Angie and later helped her prepare the tea. All this time Timothy would be shuffling through the house, opening cupboards, rooting in drawers, running his hands under the old Phillips radio; always searching, a mystified look on his face.

After tea, if there was Rosary or Benediction at the church, Sunny would attend with Angie who was the parish organist. They'd be alone in the choir gallery, Sunny gazing down on the worshipers, wondering who was praying and who was dreaming; Angie at the keyboard, a scarf tied around her head like an aviator's cap. She looked straight into space, face full of fantasy, as if driving some huge machine. Angie passed into another world when she revved up the organ, sometimes whirling out streams of consciousness long after service ended. Stained glass windows glazed by the moon on a winter's night, the smell of quenched candles, Angie and Sunny floating above the stars. Father White often had to flash the church lights, like a barman does at closing time, to get them to go home.

Before she was church organist, Angie played piano and sang with Jack O'Donnell's Orchestra, a local quintet which played weddings and dances around the county. That stopped when Timothy's mother died: he couldn't bear to be alone in the house at night, couldn't sleep if his wife was out late. Angie stood by her husband, stepped off the stage and stayed at home. As a tonic, once a week or so, Jack O'Donnell and James Grimes would drop by and they'd play for hours in the sitting room, while Timothy made tea and sandwiches in the kitchen. Sunny loved those nights: Angie on the piano, Jack O'Donnell playing saxophone and James Grimes on fiddle, bouncing out fox-trots and quick-steps to a room of invisible dancers. Every now and again a drummer would come along, a thin, dark-haired man with a crooked eye.

And sometimes, like at Christmas or holiday time, loads more musicians turned up and the hooley went on till morning. The sitting-room would be blue with cigarette smoke, everyone blasting away to beat the band and drinking like fish. That's where Sunny first tasted drink, a lukewarm hot whiskey someone had forgotten about. She took to it easily, the sweet almost medicinal taste, the hint of lemon and cloves, and the afterglow that warmed her cheeks. Later she found another one on the kitchen table and when she had it finished, she felt the unforgettable buzz. A night between Christmas and New Year's Eve, freezing hard outside and she was the merriest girl in the house.

A few weeks later, her father clattered her when he caught her making a hot whiskey in the bathroom at home. Bawling her heart out she fled up the street in the snow, blood pumping from her nose. She pounded on Angie's door and when Timothy opened it, she rushed past him and into the kitchen to her aunt. Sunny refused to go back home and stayed in the spare room for at least a month, praying that Angie might adopt her. It was a happy month. Angie explained to her the rudiments of music, introduced her to the piano and set out to teach the girl all she knew.

"She's the daughter I never had," she snapped at her husband when he grumbled about all the attention being feted on the stray child.

And then Sunny's father did a strange thing: he bought his daughter a guitar for her birthday. She cautiously returned home, like the prodigal daughter, but lodged the guitar at Angie's.

There was nobody in the county who taught the instrument and Sunny was convinced a cruel joke had been played on her. Then Angie spotted a small advertisement in the Independent —*Learn the Guitar by Mail! Play "Red River Valley" in two weeks with Victor Berginstein's New Method*. Angie wrote away for the information on Mr. Berginstein's Method and mulled over it for a week before subscribing to his correspondence course. It worked out great and between them, Angie and Mr. Berginstein had Sunny bashing out "Red River Valley" in ten days. The girl took to the instrument like a duck to water and Jack O'Donnell whispered that she was a natural.

By the following Christmas she had a stock of carols and seasonal songs and herself and a few mates busked at the turkey markets in town. The music stopped when her father bawled from his car that he'd make a necklace out of her guitar if she didn't go home and stop annoying the people. That was a nightmare Christmas. The house was a den of drunks. Her brothers were back from England for the first time since they'd left home and they weren't boys anymore, but hungry, thirsty, obnoxious young men with bulging wallets. When her father knocked over the tree on Saint Stephen's Day a brawl broke out and she retreated to her aunt's house again.

Sunny dreamed that maybe Angie and herself would start a band. At night in her bed, she'd lay awake in the blue light, conjuring up combos with Jack O'Donnell, Mattie Tracy, Toba Quin, the drummer with the squint. That winter she got lost in the guitar, playing for hours in front of the wardrobe mirror in her room. Going through numbers in the sitting-room with Angie. Writing out the words of songs. Hoping someone would come to the door with a saxophone or a fiddle. Even a drum.

Sunny played her first gig when she was sixteen. It was a fund-raiser for a new parish church and Jack O'Donnell asked if she'd like to join the orchestra for the night. They rehearsed in Angie's sitting-room for a few weeks and eventually the excitement got so frenzied that Angie announced she'd play with them on the big night, and to hell with Timothy and his phobias. Everybody chuckled and Jack O'Donnell said,

"Speak of the devil," as Timothy stooped through the door, laden down with a big tray of sandwiches.

It all seemed so long ago now. Angie bought her a black velvet dress and white blouse for the occasion. On the night, she drank a naggon of vodka before going to the hall and felt airy. They were on stage an hour before the doors opened, tinkering with microphones, testing, testing. The guitar was amplified and it was hard to get used to its sound. Angie smiled and vamped a handful of chords on the piano to stretch her fingers. The drummer with the squint did a few rolls; Grimes tuned his fiddle; the banjo player plonk-a-plonked and Jack twiddled on the saxophone. Then the doors opened with a rattle and people filed in until the smell of perfume and after-shave lotion filled the small hall. Jack O'Donnell stubbed out his cigarette and said to the orchestra,

"Nice and easy now, two sharps, 3-4 time. Away we go."

And that was it, in a few seconds the floor waltzed with dancers. Sunny's eyes followed them from the stage, watched their heads bobbing to the beat as they circled the hall like balls in a whirlpool. They smiled at her as they passed and her confidence improved as the night went on.

After the dance a few people came to congratulate Sunny on her debut and Angie introduced more who wondered who she was and what type of instrument she played. When the band had tea and ham sandwiches in the back room, Father White joined them, wedging between Angie and herself. She didn't know what to do when he put his hand on her knee and gently squeezed it. Then he moved up her thigh, talking at the top of his voice about what a great job they all had done that night. It was weird, but it gave her a bit of a zing. She didn't know if he was grabbing her for himself or Mother Church. And for weeks afterwards, she was tortured with guilt that it was she, and not he, who had sinned. Father White, Jesus Christ, sighed Sunny. And Angie left him a note...a plea for clemency? Father White really couldn't deprive her of that. After all, she had been part and parcel of his show for decades, rambling away like an organist at a silent movie.

The barman put a pint in front of her and said,
    "That's from the gentleman down the counter."
    "Huh?"
    "The gentleman down the counter."
    "Oh. Thanks."
    Sunny nodded to the man and he doffed his cap. MJ Foyle. She knew him from the Irish bars, a man in his late fifties, one of those Irish building workers who came here as a youth and never went back. Never married. He was wearing a blue suit and white open neck shirt, probably coming from evening Mass at the yellow wooden church up the road. A tubby man with a ruddy face and big innocent eyes, he raised his drink in a toast to her.
    "MJ," she smiled, "thanks for the pint."
    He nodded and turned back to the tropical fish.

60

The day herself and Borg were here, she must have stared for hours at those fish, naming them, talking to them in whale sounds. That was a good day. Borg had come over to her place the previous evening to borrow a guitar and he stayed the night. The next day, they took LSD and glided around San Francisco like kites. They were here about this time of evening and it was nearly empty, like now. They sat at the counter where MJ was sitting. Then Borg played the guitar and Sunny sang until the barman pleaded with them to leave.

She'd lost track of Borg, hadn't seen him for over a year. He stopped calling around when he hooked up with a lady from Berkeley who dealt cocaine. Pity, she liked him, they were lovers once. Well not lovers in the classic sense: they hung out together and made love nine times. She counted and even marked the calendar. And he just drifted away.

Her heart thudded when she remembered Borg never returned a guitar she loaned him: the Hofner guitar Angie bought her when she joined the Silver Stars. She got agitated, lit a cigarette, upset her drink.Jesus! She'd forgotten all about that guitar. When Borg unhooked, he took her guitar with him. She kept meaning to retrieve it, but he never returned her calls and she eventually gave up leaving messages for him. What was his telephone number? It was in the directory. He managed an apartment block near Market Street, Alpine Villas or something.

Borg's number was engaged and she stood by the phone, gazed upon by a stuffed pelican. She dialed again after a minute or two. Engaged. At least he's at home, she thought and returned to the counter. She called a brandy for herself and a pint for MJ.

Brandy was her father's drink. He was Angie's brother and drank cognac day and night while he drove around the countryside hawking insurance policies and money plans. He was drunk solid for the first seventeen years of her life and then he fell from grace and shamed them all. It happened one grey Thursday evening in March. Sunny was cycling home from school when she saw a crowd standing around the monument in the town square. The police car was there, so was the fire engine, the ambulance and Father White's black Volkswagen. When she got closer she could see there had been an accident, a car was mounted on the steps of the monument. Firemen were trying to cut the driver from the wreckage and she heard someone ask in a whisper,

"Who is it?"

"Pappy Horan," a man said.

It boomed in her ears. Pappy had rammed the monument in broad daylight. Sunny backed away and went up to Angie. For ten days she refused to go outside the door, wouldn't go to school, wouldn't go to church.

When the newspaper printed a picture of Pappy's car riding the steps like a wreck in a movie, the caption read: Lucky Escape for Ballygale man. Six months later the same photo appeared but the caption read: Jail for Ballygale man. Not alone was he drunk and delirious, but he had no insurance. Then it was discovered that nobody else in the town or neighboring parishes had insurance either. Not even Father White nor Sergeant Malone, nor Benjy Mack the court clerk or old Ma Whelan the mid-wife. And their Blue Chip Bonds and pension plans were pure junk, not worth the paper they were written on. Pappy had fiddled the barony for brandy and the law threw him in jail for two years. It broke him, he aged decades and never drank again. Never did anything again except pray, pray, pray.

She hopped from her seat and bounced to the phone, bangles jingling, heels clicking. Still engaged. Sunny bit her lip. Who's he talking to? Maybe the phone is off the hook, or there's something wrong with the line. She asked the operator to check it.

"That line's fine, caller. There's a conversation on that line."

"Thank you operator, I'll try it again."

"You do that. Have a nice weekend, caller."

Nice weekend my ass. At least he's at home. She had to get that guitar back. Maybe best to get a cab up to his place. It can't be too far...up Thirteenth Street or whatever you call it and left on Market. That's what she'd do, get a cab there before he left for the night.

It was a quick ride to Church and Market and Sunny got out across the street from Borg's place. Twilight was creeping from the east and gusts of night-wind whirled litter and dust in the air. Cars sped left and right, propelled by anticipation: Saturday night in San Francisco, Bangkok of the West. The shops were shut and the homeless were taking over the doorways with their supermarket carts of junk and clothes, street-soiled sleeping bags and cardboard cabins.

She climbed the steps to Borg's apartment building, anger and alcohol pumping her steps. God help Borg if he hasn't got my guitar. She pressed his bell once, twice, three times. Immediately the door buzzed and she pushed it open.

Junk mail covered the hall floor: pizza coupons, missing children cards, newsletters, parking tickets, invitations to church. The place was grubby, dimly lit and much more rundown than she remembered it. Trotting upstairs the spicy smell of Indian curry hung in the air like temple incense. On the first floor she heard snatches of John Lennon, Vanilla Ice and Joni Mitchell. On the next she heard mantras, Bob Dylan, Madonna and a domestic squabble.

Borg lived on the top floor and as she approached his flat the air got ranker. He had the door open before she had a chance to knock.

"Christ! Sunny! I was expecting someone else..." he said in alarm, turning and rushing into the kitchen, "come in...sit down somewhere. Pardon the mess, I'm just tidying the place. What's up?"

"I won't be delaying," she said, looking around the living - room for a somewhere to sit. The place was chaotic. Clothes thrown everywhere, mounds of them, dirty and forgotten. Months of newspapers and heaps of bulging black refuse bags against the walls. The coffee table was covered with dirty cups and glasses, beer cans and milk cartons. In one corner, a bedraggled green parrot pecked its shoulder and squawked around a filthy cage. There was bird shit all over the television, streaks of it on the screen. Borg was talking to her from the bathroom, a hundred words a minute. She couldn't understand what he was saying over the noise of running water and the squawking parrot.

Sunny cleared a space on the black sofa under the window, sat down and scanned the room for her guitar. All the shelves were bare. The stereo was gone and so was the psychedelic light machine. Not a single tape or record in the racks, even the pictures were gone from the wall. His keyboard wasn't to be seen and neither was her guitar. I hope the fucker hasn't pawned it, she thought, staring at four black flies hovering in formation, circling under the light bulb. The long glass case where the tortoises lived was smashed and she wondered if they were on the floor somewhere. Then she noticed something crawl from under the table: the rabbit, Rodger, a piebald creature with flopped ears. She remembered him from the last time she was here, but he seemed sadder now, scrawny and forlorn.

Sunny lit a cigarette and looked for an ashtray. She found one on the floor beside a small mirror and a red and white McDonald's straw: Cocaine itsy bitsys. Then she noticed more paraphernalia on a dinner plate...dark stained tin foil, matches, safety razor.

"Oh that," chuckled Borg, striding into the room, "I had a visit from the muse last night."

"Oh yeah?"

Close up, she was taken aback at how wasted he had gotten. Just flesh and bone. Borg busied himself picking up things and leaving them down again. Frowning at the blank walls. Scratching his neck. Yawning nervously. Wired. Skid row on the top floor.

"I see you're playing at Rita's Place next week," he babbled, "things are going well."

An opening.

"Yeah, that's why I'm here...Borg, I need that guitar of mine you borrowed. The semi-acoustic Hofner."

"A Hofner?" Borg shook his head and walked towards the parrot, muttering:

"Guitar? Hofner? Semi-acoustic?"

She retraced the day of the loan for him, their visit to Jonah's Bark, returning here with a bottle of tequila and two burritos.

"Yeah," he said, "vaguely, vaguely...but as far as I remember,

65

I brought the guitar back to you."

"No Borg."

"Yeah, remember...I brought it down to you the night you played The Sheehan."

"No Borg, you never brought back that guitar. You never even bothered to return my calls."

"Look, there's been a lot going on in my life..."

The doorbell rang and he leaped like a cat and buzzed the ringer in.

"Look Sunny," he said anxiously, "this is not cool...this is not a cool time to call."

"Borg, I'm not leaving without my fucking guitar."

"Well it's not here Sunny."


While Borg did business with his dealer, she stayed in the bathroom. It stank with a fetid, fishy smell and she turned on the fan and opened the window. Smell or no smell she was holding out here. She stared in disgust at the boat-shaped mound in the bath which was covered by a fallen shower curtain. She saw it move and wondering what was under it, she lifted the curtain and gasped. The bath was full of stranded tortoises and turtles, abandoned and forgotten. On their backs lay a guitar case, like they were carrying it somewhere.

"Jesus Christ, that's like mine."

She grabbed the case, laid it on the bathroom floor and flicked the clasps. There it was, like a corpse in a casket, the Hofner guitar Angie had bought her. Sunburst body, ebony finger board with mother of pearl inlay.

Kneeling down, she took it from it's purple velvet bed and

strummed a chord. Still in tune, it filled the white tiled room and she strummed another chord and another still. Life makes no sense she thought, tortoises in the bath, suicides in the cowhouse, junkies in the sitting-room. She heard Angie's voice, the thumping piano, the saxophone, fiddle and drum. Hot tears blurred her eyes and Sunny beat out blue chords and let her heart flow into a song.

# THE STAR OF MADRABAWN

THE NINE O' CLOCK NEWS WAS OVER AND Mrs. Keogh switched off the radio before the sports results were read.

"No news," she said quietly and glanced at Spoke Whelan, her lone lodger.

"No mention," he said, neatly folding a newspaper by the fire, "And the winners were to be announced last week, what ever is the delay."

She put a shovel of coal in the  fire and ventured,

"But then again, they say that no news is good news."

"No news is good news," repeated Spoke in a whisper tainted with despair.

"But maybe the judges in Dublin haven't tested the inventions yet."

"Dublin is Ireland."

Mrs Keogh nodded in sympathetic agreement and turned away to boil the kettle. She felt responsible for his angst. He wouldn't have entered the *Inventor of the Year* competition if she hadn't suggested it.

Not that she thought he had a chance of winning, she just wanted to get the invention out of the house.

Spoke had lodged with Mrs. Keogh for nearly fifteen years and worked in the shop at the front of the house, where her late husband had sold paint and wallpaper. Though technically a bicycle mechanic, he was easily lured into other fields of technology when people took their troubles to him. He hadn't the heart to ever refuse a job, no matter how complicated or alien it might be. During surgery, it might dawn on him how something could function better and from the chaos came totally new inventions. Hair dryers became egg cookers; washing machines turned into jukeboxes; vacuum cleaners re-birthed as paint sprayers. Often customers were not satisfied with his transformations and cat-fights erupted in the workshop. Mrs. Keogh wished he'd stick with simple bicycles.

The invention he entered in the Department of Enterprise and Trade competition had disturbed Mrs. Keogh. The brain-wave for it came when Spoke wondered *what if you crossed a hot water bottle with an electric kettle?* After a few weeks of research and development, he showed Mrs. Keogh a leather skinned mattress filled with water and heated by six electric elements. He encouraged her to sit on it and she did.

"God but it's very comfortable."

"And great to sleep on," grinned Spoke, sitting beside her, "Real comfort."

When he leaned back a little, the mattress quivered and Mrs. Keogh hopped off like a rabbit.

"Go aisey in case you burst it!" she warned.

"What burst?" he laughed, "you could trot an ass on this! What burst? Is it coddin' me you are Kitty?"

That was as familiar as he ever got to her in all those years.

"I'll make the next wan for you Kitty," he said, "This is the prototype."

"The prototype," Mrs. Keogh said slowly, disliking the taste of the word.

The prototype stalked Mrs. Keogh and she dreamed it turned into a monstrous blob that consumed the house. She woke up crying for Spoke and was relieved to hear him snoring down the hall. Another night she dreamed she was tied naked to the prototype and Spoke was walking around in a white toga, reciting what she thought was a Black Mass. Like help from Heaven, a few days later she read about the competition in the paper. She showed him the piece and urged,

"Send them the prototype, it's your best invention yet."


Mrs. Keogh got up to brew a pot of tea, but stopped mid-stride, like she had a cramp.

"Do you know something," she said hazily, "I had a dream about you last night. It's only after coming to me now."

"Is that so?"

"You were after discovering something—it was something important because there was a big crowd around you."

She stood by the table and recalled the dream in patches, cutting and pasting it into sequence. Mrs. Keogh thought Spoke had discovered a new star. His eyebrows arched.

"It caused great commotion," she said with authority, "there was a huge crowd of people below at Murphy's Corner and you were looking through a long yoke and it was pointed at the sky over Madrabawn. I s'pose it was some class of an eye-glass or other— but in the dream it was like wan of these old cannon guns."

Spoke nodded: you could indeed see Madrabawn from Murphy's Corner. He smiled and thawed a little. But why the cannon gun? Spaceships maybe.

"I think it's a good omen for the invention," she said.

"Hah-hah-hah," he chuckled, scratching the back of his neck, "Anything is possible. Anything is possible."

Spoke wondered about her dream: she had odd ones, but he always felt they meant something if you could decipher them. He'd read somewhere that you could interpret dreams by role-playing, but usually Mrs. Keogh's were too complex for that. This one seemed straight-forward enough and he ran through it in his head again. He finished his tea and blessed himself.

"I'll ramble down the town and see if there's anything stirrin'—I'll be back in a while."

"Do," she encouraged, "the walk 'll do you good."

On the way out he went to the workshop and rooted a large black box from the junk. He covered it with his overcoat and went down Church Street.

It was a clear night and every star in the heavens shimmered. The town was still, the dark grey footpaths brightened here and there by patches of light from empty public houses. Cats scrapped in Boland's Lane and a dog barked in a yard. A baby cried in the bowels of a house and a drunk argued with himself in a dark alley. The bell of the Protestant Church pealed ten and Spoke peered up and down the deserted street before crossing to Murphy's Corner.

In the shadows of Clare Street, he opened the box and set up an old astronomy telescope belonging to the late Major Tubelo. He spread the limbs of the tripod and the steel tips grated on the flag footpath. Then a metal adjuster slipped from his hand and clanged on the ground. The noise attracted the attention of Cissy Casey who was rubbing night-cream on her face. She peeped through the curtains and called her husband Dan.

"What's Spoke doin?" she asked.

"The dirty scut," hissed Dan, "he's lookin' at Nono Hogan strip through a spyglass."

Uaigneas Gallagher left Wally's Bar after playing tunes all night to nobody. Fiddle-case under his left arm, he eased down Main Street until he spotted the police car at Murphy's corner. Uaigneas retreated into the shadows and listened to the Law squabbling with Spoke Whelan. He saw the writhing mechanic being bundled into the lawmobile, his contraption contemptuously thrown in the trunk. Gallagher stood still as the patrol car drove away in a swirl of blue and orange flashes.

When calm returned, Uaigneas walked across the square to a long black van, reminiscent of a hearse with its side windows and solemn forehead. Erased letters on the doors read: *U. Gallagher, Undertaker*. Spoke's handiwork. The bicycle mechanic had been contracted to convert  the hearse to a passenger wagon when Uaigneas lost his vocation.

It took a while for the engine to fire and then Uaigneas let it warm up, revving the accelerator erratically until the vehicle filled with blue fumes. He awkwardly turned in the square before switching on the lights. On the third attempt he crunched into second gear and slowly climbed uphill to Church Street.

Mrs. Keogh was raking the fire for the night when she heard a vehicle stop outside. While wondering who it might be, she was jolted by a sudden ring of the bell Spoke had recently installed. She opened the door and was surprised to see Uaigneas Gallagher, a former lodger.

"Good night, Mrs. Keogh...t'is cool."

"T'is. But thank God there's no rain."

"I'm afraid Mr. Whelan is in a bit of bother."

"Oh? Come in let you."

Uaigneas sat at the kitchen table and she made a pot of tea. He had been drinking, she could smell it. But he hadn't too much taken. Pouring him a cup of tea she asked,

"And what word have you about Mr. Whelan?"

"I'm afraid he got arrested," Uaigneas said, slowly spooning sugar into his cup.

"Oh Sweet Jesus!"

For a few seconds Mrs. Keogh seemed to swoon, wavering the tea pot over his lap. She sat down and fanned her face with a handkerchief while Uaigneas told of Spoke's arrest.

"And the sergeant called him a pervert."

The word reminded her of the prototype.

"He'll be the talk of the country," she whispered.

Uaigneas looked around the kitchen and noticed it had been painted since he was last in the house. There was a picture of the new Pope over the radio and two black and white porcelain dogs on the dresser.

"The place is lookin' smashin'," he said.

"You haven't been here for a long time, sure. Not since yourself and Mr. Whelan fell out."

"He can be very cranky."

"That's the brains, he's rotting with brains."

"Do you think he knew about the arrangement?"

Mrs. Keogh didn't expect the question and ruffled in her chair. She looked at Uaigneas, looked at the fire.

"He never mentioned it," she muttered, "will...will you have another drop of tea?"

Uaigneas passed his cup. The tea was strong and bitter and he only sipped it. Mrs Keogh fanned herself with the handkerchief again, she was warm and her clothes felt tight. It was years since they had an arrangement, years since she let him share her bed. Years since Spoke and himself fell-out over the conversion of the hearse. It was a botched job and when Uaigneas refused to pay up, Spoke threatened him with an electric branding iron. Mrs. Keogh was upset when he left her lodgings: he had been a good counter-weight to Spoke and the arrangement suited her. On a practical level, he was always late with the rent and months in arrears when he bailed out. He mailed her back the door key, wrapped in a five-pound note.

"You know, it's funny that you called. I was only dreaming about you last night."

"Really?"

"You were playing the fiddle...right here in the kitchen... there was a crowd of people here and television cameras and everything. I think you were famous."

He made no comment and she wondered if she'd told him that dream before sometime. He was looking at the clock over the fireplace, an anguished twist on his face.

"It's getting late," she said, "maybe you should stay the night rather than driving back to Madrabawn."

"I suppose it might be better."

"And you could park the hearse in the back lane. It's not a great sign to see one outside a house in the morning."

While he moved the vehicle, Mrs. Keogh filled two hot water bottles and gave thanks to Saint Martin. She sprinkled the bedroom with rosewater and tucked her dream-book under the mattress.

# Flying Visit

At the after-show party, a slender fair-haired woman in buckskin jacket waited while Kevin Cawley signed autographs and shook hands with well-wishers. Lead dancer with the Heart of Ireland show, he was red haired, well shaped and in his thirties.

"Hi," she said quietly, "you were great tonight."

"Thanks. Are you a performer yourself?"

"No, I'm a film-maker, documentaries."

Kevin nodded, offered her a can of beer. He sensed a film opportunity as she asked questions about dancing and music in Ireland.

She smiled when he smiled. Kevin touched her shoulder and said,

"I'm sorry, what did you say your name was?"

"Wendy, Wendy Torrance."

Kevin and Wendy had supper in a quiet diner off Broadway. He heard she'd made an award-winning film on the Hopi Indians and another about the salmon fisheries of the North-West Coast. Kevin told her he was a baker back in Ireland and the Heart tour was the first time he'd ever left the country. After two more weeks in New York, he'd be back in the hot house.

"I'd be happy to show you around the city while you're here," she offered.

"I'd like that," Kevin said and clasped her hand to seal the deal.

Wendy lived in Brooklyn, in a brownstone house decorated with Native American furniture and weavings, stacks of pine bookshelves and Mayan paintings. Her bedroom was large and serene, low lights, soft flute music weaving through sage and cedar incense. A feather bed with a cosy duvet, Kevin waited between the covers while she showered.

After love-making they lay entwined and he fingered her soft fair hair.

"You know," he muttered, "I should have told you... I'm married."

"I guessed that."

He spoke about his wife and two kids and Wendy said she'd been married once but it didn't work out. Kevin indicated his own marriage was rocky, a bit love-less. She held his hand to her cheek and tucked the duvet around his freckled shoulders.

Kevin danced even better the following night and departed the stage with the audience on their feet. After the show he left the auditorium by a side door and Wendy took him off to supper in her green Volvo. Later they returned to the brownstone house in Brooklyn and talked and made love until dawn brightened the bedroom.

New York exhilarated him. Noise and bustle, smell of delis, smoke from pubs, streaking taxis, screaming cop cars. Kevin and Wendy held hands and she brought him to her favorite places; her heart warmed at the awe in his face as he gazed up at skyscrapers and towers. They strolled around Greenwich Village and St. Mark's Square, embraced by the Hudson, bought toys for his kids at F.A.O. Swartz. He never felt happier and wondered if he was falling in love, but dismissed the thought, reasoning it could never happen so quick.

After a few days, his show-mates noticed a change in Kevin. They remarked how affable he'd become, how well he looked. And most of all how great he danced. Reviewers raved about him. One called him King of the Dancers and his arrival on stage was awaited with palpable anticipation by the audience. His performance brought them to their feet and fans teemed backstage afterwards to meet him. But he was always gone before they got there, away with Wendy for supper and more. His room-mate, singer Hawley Hannigan, told the troupe Kevin had moved his gear out of the hotel.

A week with Wendy, Kevin was enjoying himself so much that he wanted to stay in New York for an extra few days after the show closed. He told the tour manager of his plans and asked if his flight home could be changed. The manager said he'd check it out and Kevin patted him on the back and gave him Wendy's phone number in case he needed to contact him.

Sunday morning, Kevin and Wendy were lounging in bed, watching television, when the phone rang. She answered and passed the receiver to him.

"What the fuck are you doing with that bitch?" his wife Majella lashed.

"What?" blurted Kevin, swinging out of bed.

"Get out of there you bloody fucker before I fly over and drag you out..."

Kevin was flabbergasted. Stood naked in the kitchen, hands criss-crossing his chest. Wendy made coffee but he couldn't drink it. He began to shiver and she got a dressing gown and draped it over his shoulders.

"I'm sorry," she whispered.

He nodded and put her hands on his face. They went back to bed and lay in silence, stared at the ceiling.

That night before the show, he tackled the tour manager. I didn't know it was your wife, the manager said, Hawley Hannigan put her call through to my room. When he cornered Hannigan, the singer pleaded,

"What could I do? She called for the last two mornings looking for you."

"And why didn't you tell me?" Kevin cried.

"I forgot..."

"Only for you're going on stage, I'd break your fucking face."


Kevin didn't dance well and left the theater immediately after his performance, not even bothering to wait for the encore. Instead of supper in the little diner, he drank whiskey in a Soho bar, Wendy beside him, sipping a glass of white wine. Conversation was sparse and when they returned to her place, Kevin quickly glided into drunken sleep. She held him in her arms, shielded him from nightmares and Irish hexes.

The phone woke them next morning and when Majella asked for her husband, Wendy politely said there was nobody there by that name. Kevin closed his eyes in agony and tears dribbled down his face.

"I hate going back," he said quietly, "I hate leaving you Wendy."

"You do what you feel is right," she whispered.

Wendy brought him to the airport and waited while he checked in for the flight to Ireland with the rest of the Heart troupe. Boarding pass in hand, Kevin met her in the bar and they smiled sadly at each other. She took a tiny box from her handbag.

"A little gift for you," she said, "Indian beads."

He nodded, thanked her with a kiss.

"If you ever get to America again, please contact me," Wendy said.

Shuffling down the crowded aisle of the plane, Kevin clenched his teeth, like he was psyching himself up for the murderous row with Majella that loomed on the other side. He found his seat between Hannigan and Kelly, threw his bag in the overhead bin and sat down. Passengers filed through the aisles, air stewards swished by, his stage mates thumbed through inflight magazines. Kevin stared at the back of the seat in front of him, battling surges of sadness and panic. Suddenly he unbuckled the safety belt, left his seat and hurried to the front of the plane. Two flight attendants stood at the door and he rushed past them.

"Sir! Sir!" they called as he hurried up the loading tunnel and back into the terminal. Officials called after him but he kept going, breaking into a run, past gates, lounges, bars and coffee carts. They tried to stop him at the security check but Kevin leaped over the barrier and headed to an airport exit. Passengers scurried out of his way, cops cried after him. One shouted,

"Stop or I'll shoot!"

He pushed through the glass exit door and ran outside. Neither looking left or right, he bolted across the road and was spun in the air by a speeding taxi.

Unable to get any information from the unconscious fugitive, the police could not rule out a terrorist plot. They ordered all luggage to be unloaded and checked; passengers had to disembark while the plane was swept by security men and sniffer dogs. After five hours the flight was cleared for take-off and Kevin Cawley lay in the Hebrew Hospital, his two legs suspended from the ceiling. Next day, the Irish newspapers carried the story with a photo of Kevin. The country wondered what came over the champion dancer. In the end, they put it down to fear of flying and prayed him a speedy recovery.

When Kevin regained consciousness he couldn't figure out where he was or what had happened to him. His head was bandaged and he couldn't feel his legs, though he saw them hanging before him. His hands had feeling and he was connected to a bank of monitors and grey steel cases with lights and dials.

"Oh God," he moaned and drifted away again.

Next time he came around, a nurse was taking his pulse and she smiled at his bloodshot eyes.

"You're doing good," she said and he nodded.

Majella called from Ireland and a nurse brought the phone to Kevin. He wasn't able to talk, words broke in his throat. She spoke curtly and without sympathy, asked if he'd thought about suing the taxi company. Cards and flowers came from family, friends and well-wishers. Detectives interviewed him when he was stronger. He couldn't explain why he left the plane, pure panic maybe, he told them. They nodded and left. A man from the Irish embassy heard the same story. Then Wendy was allowed to visit and his spirits lifted. They held hands over the bedclothes and he whispered that he loved her: it really hit him when he sat on the plane, he wasn't able to face going back. Their hands gripped tighter and tears flowed down their faces.

Every few days Majella phoned, often when Wendy was in the room and Kevin became an emotional yo-yo, depressed one minute, love-struck the next. As his body regained strength, his heart and mind became more tormented. Some days he wished to stay in New York with Wendy; other days he wept for his kids; more days he felt Majella reeling him back like a fish.

In the end, Kevin decided to return to Ireland and to his family. Wendy agreed to accompany him on the flight over, take the next one back to New York. An ambulance brought them from the hospital to the airport and flight staff looked warily at him as he hobbled down the aisle on crutches. Wendy settled him in the seat and sat alongside. He was pale and nervous, gripped her hands while the plane taxied for take-off.

When the bar opened he ordered a whiskey and Wendy had water. Not much was said between them until Kevin had a few more drinks. Then he told her he had never met anyone as loving or as kind as her, and she deserved someone a lot better than him.

"I'll never dance again," he whispered, "I'm just a cripple now."

"That's not true," she said, "You'll be back dancing in no time."

He shook his head and pressed the attendant's bell for another drink.

Half-way over the Atlantic, Kevin needed to go to the bathroom. He was drunk and Wendy helped him from the seat, put the crutches under his arms and guided him to the toilet. She pushed the door open and eased him inside.

"You'll need to come in and help me," he said.

She did, closed the door behind and took the crutches while he steadied himself with one hand, tried opening his fly with the other. He relieved himself and said,

"We should make love one last time."

They tried. Kevin sat on the toilet and Wendy straddled him. She coaxed him best she could but soon his legs hurt and she had to dismount.

"We should get back to our seats," she said.

Kevin woke when the plane landed at Shannon. Confused, he looked through the porthole at the grey morning rain and suddenly he felt cold and began to shiver. Wendy was already out of her seat and had his crutches ready. At the plane door, a wheelchair was waiting, smiling attendant standing beside it. Wendy held the crutches, helped him into the chair. He looked up at her with anxious eyes and said,

"I'll be able to manage on my own from here."

She nodded, bent down and kissed him on the forehead.

"Good-bye Kevin," she whispered, "I'll miss you."

The attendant wheeled Kevin up the tunnel and into Ireland. Leaving customs he looked around as the wheelchair approached the exit door: Wendy waved his crutches. He panicked; wanted to do something, say something. The door closed behind with a creak and he entered the arrivals hall.

From a distance, Wendy watched him being wheeled through the airport terminal by Majella, flanked by two burly men, probably her brothers. She saw them exit the building, the wind ruffling Kevin's fiery red hair. A black car was parked at the kerb and the men opened doors and lifted Kevin into the back. Majella got in beside him and one of the men folded the airport wheelchair and tossed it into the trunk. Wendy watched as the car pulled away from the pavement and nosed into a slow stream of traffic.

She stepped outside the airport to get a glimpse of Ireland but inhospitable wind and rain pushed her back inside almost immediately. Wendy checked her ticket and wandered around the terminal until she found the ladies. She locked herself in a cubicle and wept, her arms wrapped around Kevin's crutches.

Later, with no more tears to cry and her mouth dry, she propped the crutches against the stall wall and kissed them goodbye. She freshened up, brushed her teeth, checked the time and went to the bar. In a small booth, away from the babbling television, Wendy drank Irish coffees and wrote in her journal until the flight to New York was called.

# BACK IN THE
## DAYS OF CORNCRAKES

ARTHUR GUINNESS PUT ME ON TELEVISION.
It happened one warm July morning, while on
my way to help John Joe Maher make hay. I saw
a film crew setting up in the town square and
went to see what they were at. Making television
ads for Guinness, a gaffer told me. Great stuff, I
thought, nothing like a bit of excitement and a
bunch of strangers to give the town a lift. And
what a great day for it. A day with butterflies and
honey bees, soft scents of summer and the far-
away sounds of hay machines.

John Joe would be interested in this: great
fodder for philosophical discussion under the
mid-day sun. I made mental notes: at least a dozen
men running around like rats, all yapping and
checking gauges and dials and cameras. A few
women in tight jeans smoked hard and dashed
here and there with clipboards and stopwatches.
Everyone wore sunglasses and bright clothes, lots
of neck scarves, jerkins and tweed caps. A fat

man, wearing a baseball cap, sat on a chair in the back of a pick-up truck and shouted at everyone. He was the director. When he saw me he roared,

"Hey you! You! What the hell are you doing over there? You should be over here!"

"Haw?"

One of the women clutched my elbow and led me to a caravan, where a few locals were fitting on white tuxedos: Gaga Murray, Paddy Logan, Stab Jordan, Matty Fullbright and Hopper Hogan. Pride of the Drinking Class. I was press ganged into the cast of the barman's race which was going to be a new television ad for Arthur Guinness. Years later my grandmother would weep that that was when I lost my innocence and began slipping downhill. But that summer's morning there was no time to object, so I donned the tux and looked around for the cameras. I was just sixteen and mad for road. You could make hay on any sunny day.

A clipboard women came around with pages of forms to sign.

"Royalties," whispered Matty Fullbright, "read everything extremely carefully."

"When do we get our money?" whined Paddy Logan.

"Sign here sir," the woman said, and he did because nobody had ever called him 'sir' before.

"Any hope of a few bottles of porter while we're waitin'?" asked Gaga Murray in the politest of voices.

"No problem," she said and called someone on a walkie-talkie. In minutes, bottles of porter were frothing, cigarettes went around and we lounged in the caravan like the Rolling Stones before a gig. The crack was mighty. I was the youngest and supped moderately, not being as used to drink as the others.

By the time the action began, the caravan was throttled with empty bottles; the lads must have downed at least two six packs each. We were hauled out into the sunlight, all eyes on us and I suddenly felt my feet go rubbery. Guards blocked off the street to traffic, the director waited for an aeroplane to pass overhead and we lined up at Healy's Corner. Six merry barmen in white coats, each carrying a tray with a bottle of Guinness and an empty glass. The director gave a countdown and on ACTION! we poured the porter into the glass like he ordered and ran with the trays balanced on one hand.

The first run was a disaster because Gaga Murray stumbled immediately and upset my tray. Porter spilled, glasses broke, and someone had to run into Healy's for a sweeping brush. Back to start. Next time was a little better, but we only got a few yards when something happened to a camera and it was 'fall out for a smoke and a bottle' time. I drank a little quicker—what else do you do with free beer, the lads encouraged, lashing it back as fast as they were able.

Paddy Logan began talking about 'agents' and 'contracts' and calculated how much we were making while we drank. Hopper asked if we could bring the tuxedos home with us and Stab wondered if this gig could affect the dole. Fullbright said we should make it last as long as we could and Gaga Murray, noticing we were running dry, called for more porter. No problem, the woman with the clipboard said.

"This is the life," whispered Gaga , "say nothin', say nothin', this is the life. Hollywood. Hollywood."

We had a third try at the race before breaking for lunch. Like the other 'shoots', this one was also a fiasco, marred (again) by Gaga who got an attack of nerves at the starting line and sprayed brown porter all over Logan's tuxedo. The director called him a 'bungler' and suggested finding a replacement. Fullbright stuck out his chest and warned,

"If you're going to replace Gaga, you'll have to replace us all. I don't give a fuck where you're from or who your mother is—but if Gaga goes, we all go."

The director was bewildered and shot quick looks at the rest of us. We played dumb. Fullbright went on,

"Anyway, we'll have to get more money to make this caper worth our while. I could be makin' hay today, instead of arsing around here waiting to do Arthur Guinness a favor."

Fullbright didn't own a blade of grass.

"More money!" screamed the director, "Jesus fella, you've already cost Guinness a fortune."

"A fortune!" yelled Fullbright, "Jesus Christ, t'is Guinness that's cost us a fortune. Cost this whole fuckin' town a fortune."

Before things got hotter, a man from the Sycamore Hotel arrived with a station-wagon full of sandwiches and dainties, tea, wine and coffee. Grub brought a cooling period and one of the women came over to our caravan while we ate and tried to reason with Fullbright who was now casting aspersions on the way things were being done. He said,

"I could shoot 'Gone With The fucking Wind' with half the crew here and still have change in my pocket."

She nodded patiently and said if he left the director alone, she'd make sure that Gaga would be fine.

"But please take it easy, you fellas. Okay?"

"I wonder," Gaga whispered to her, "would there be any

chance of gettin' another drop of wine, t'is supposed to be great for the nerves."

"No problem! Coming up! Just...just keep things cool, okay?"

"Mortal cool," whispered Gaga, winking and nodding at her, "We won't say another word,"

We got back on 'the set' around two o'clock and by that time Gaga was totally spaced. Fullbright was full, the bottled porter giving him gas problems. Paddy Logan was banjaxed, a bottle in each hand, cigarette hanging from the lips, waiting for stardom. Stab had hic-cups and Hopper Hogan was filling his pockets with salad sandwiches.

The next shoot was a farce—Gaga again. Just as the cameras rolled he got the shakes and everything on his tray rattled like a snare drum. But he couldn't move, couldn't pick up the bottle and pour it into the glass like the director was shouting at us to do. The director screamed at him.

"Pour it you dumbhead! Pour the fucking thing!"

Gaga couldn't move, just shook like a statue in an earth-quake. I thought he was going to shake himself apart and collapse into a heap.

"CUT!!!" roared the director before more film was wasted.

There was a mini-conference and Gaga and Fullbright were brought over to talk to the director who seemed to have turned purple. We could pick up some of the argument. Gaga has to go: Then we all go. Gaga is a liability: He only has a touch of stage-fright. Then he shouldn't be here: Gaga has every right to be here, this is his home town.

Fullbright wanted to call a strike and a man from the local Chamber of Commerce was dragged in to mediate. A compromise was reached: Gaga got one last chance and if he blew it, he was out of the race and the man from the Chamber of Commerce took his place. We went back to start, Gaga was propped between Stab and myself for support.

"Christ," he whimpered, "I'm burstin' to make a lake."

The director was on the countdown.

"Hang on to it," I muttered.

"ACTION!"

We grabbed the bottles, poured the porter and rushed up the street, trays balanced like waiters. Everything was dunky-dory, no problems. Fullbright and myself were leading until about half-way up the town when Gaga passed us on the inside like a rocket, Grace Lennon's psychotic poodle snapping at his heels. Gaga's body was arched like an unfortunate cartoon character and my first reaction was 'that's him gone for a burton.' But the director kept the cameras rolling and zoomed in on the chase. The crew cheered, the dog went bananas, Gaga went faster. He won the race hands down, broke through the finishing line and kept going, straight into Hassett's pub, slamming the door in the poodle's face.

When Gaga re-appeared, race won, dog gone and bladder emptied, Fullbright was shouting at the director,

"Now is Gaga a liability? Hah? You'll never get a scene like that again. Hah? Gaga is a professional. This is the real thing man. Hah? This is the real Ireland."

And so it was. Back in the days of corncrakes, and us poor peasants making Guinness ads instead of making hay.

# WAITING FOR A FARE

BRIDGEY LOONEY WAS FILLING A PINT WHEN she saw the two-tone cream and green car park in the town square. She thought it an odd-looking vehicle, curvy like a candy in Christmas box, with a taxi sign on the roof. When the driver got out and stretched himself, she almost dropped the pint: he was a foreigner with sand-coloured skin. A short man with long black hair and curly beard, he wore a grey tweed jacket over a pale ankle-length robe.

There was much whispering that day as people wondered where the new cabby came from, what make of car he drove.

"He's a Pakistani," Moll Tobin said, "I used see them in London."

An Indian, Pat Carroll guessed but John Hartigan the cobbler thought he came from Nepal or maybe Tibet. Mrs. Hogan the church organist said he was like one of the Magi who paid homage to the infant Jesus in the manger and suggested there was no harm in him.

He stayed till late and seemed cheerful when leaving, though he collected no fare. Early next morning when Bridgey opened the bar, he was back again, reading a newspaper spread on the car bonnet. She noticed he was wearing a different jacket and thought she saw the glint of an earring through his black hair. He collected no fare that day or the next but the sun shone brighter and warmer than it had in years and Bridgey thought,

"Well at least he brought the good weather with him."

After a week without customers, people thought he'd go away and when he didn't, some grew agitated. Peter Berry, a conservative draper, said he was a 'quare hawk' and doubted the man was fully insured or held a valid driving license. He mentioned his suspicions to Sergeant Malone and a few days later the policeman approached the cab.

"Viry hoppy to meet you, offy-sur," the driver smiled with outstretched hand.

Malone observed he wore a wrist of blue-green bangles and a gold ring with a big ruby. But his papers were all in order. So were his indicators, brake lights, hooter, tyres. The policeman checked everything in the car except oil and water.

"And what's his name?" Peter Berry asked the sergeant when they met for a drink that night.

"Manji Jadpul or something."

"Jesus Christ," Berry hissed, "if I had to walk from here to Russia but I wouldn't travel with him."

A month passed and nobody patronized Manji Jadpul, but he arrived every morning and parked in the middle of the square. They wondered where he went at night, if he had a family. Bridgey Looney noticed he brought lunch with him and ate in the car. One day she got the whiff of aromatic spices and saw him stir a saucepan over a camping gas stove beside the taxi. The smell got strong as rabbit stew and lay on the town for hours after. Lala Logan thought it smelled like curry she had once in Liverpool and it reminded Ray Flynn of ban-gang he'd ate in Hong Kong after the last war. Coyne the butcher said the smell would knock a horse and came from no meat he knew of. Peter Berry put a tissue to his nose and claimed it was a bad sign to see the foreigner cooking on the street: he was really settling in.

"And mark my words," Coyne nodded, "next we'll see more of them landing in town."

This bothered Berry and his jaw twitched. Coyne then whispered that Manji might be a 'homo' or a queer.

"Well he's some sort of a sexual anyway," Peter Berry agreed, "cause no right man would dress like that."

When Mary Delaney had to go visit her mother in Foxhill, she glanced anxiously at the taxi from her house. For an hour she stood behind the lace curtain, wondering if she'd hire him. It was a terribly public act and it took a decade of the Rosary to shift her qualms. Leaving the house, she blessed herself with Holy Water. There was not another soul on the street, but she felt the eyes of the town watching her and her breathing got heavy. As she approached the car, Manji hopped out and bowed. Mary balked. The color of his skin, his shimmering silk robe and smell of sweet cologne overwhelmed her. She briskly veered away and crossed to Casey's shop and bought a newspaper.

Sam Callahan, the street sweeper, got close to the taxi one afternoon and even said hello to Manji. The driver greeted hello and something that sounded to Sam like: *Who invented water?* He shook his head, drew a blank and gazed at the book on Manji's lap.

Sam tried to read the title but couldn't. It was in strange writing, he told Bridgey Looney when he went for a pint after work. She nodded and said that men from the East were very brainy. Callahan had a swallow of porter.

"Jesus Bridgey," he said, "if I'd anyplace to go to but I'd hire the poor hure."

"You would sure," she agreed, "t'would even be worth finding somewhere to go to, to give the cratur a few shillings. Even if three or four people got together and went on a pilgrimage to Knock, wouldn't it be something for him."

"Now you're talkin' Bridgey."

All that summer Manji came to town seven days a week and left empty handed. And yet he smiled through, riding home to strange music weaving from his car. One evening, just outside the town, Hacksaw Casey hitched a ride and Manji stopped, tyres screeching. Casey cautiously approached the car and asked,

"Are you goin' towards Lavahossle?"

"Sorry I do not know the way there....but I'll be pleased to take you."

"That's grand," Casey mumbled and backed away from the car which he later said smelled like a perfume factory.

On hearing Casey's experience, Coyne the butcher pronounced that Manji was not a taxi if he didn't know the way to Lavahossle. Even a blind man could find Lavahossle, he announced with a sharp twitch of the head. Martin Coffey agreed and Harry Considine suggested it was time to urge Manji out of town. But it will have to be done discreetly, Peter Berry whispered. For a couple of nights they huddled in the back room of Dodo Ryan's bar, muttering like members of a secret society. The plan came to Berry while he relieved himself in the lavatory and when he told the others, they clapped him on the shoulders. Later, bellies full of porter, they crept to the square and laid a carpet of two inch nails where they figured Manji parked. The job took an hour, each nail-head set in the tar.

"That'll fix him," whispered Coyne and they stood back and admired the spikes.

They were at their windows next morning when the taxi arrived in the square. Manji parked, got out and laid a newspaper on the bonnet and began to read. Berry hurried down the street to Coyne and said in disbelief,

"Nothing happened."

"The little bastard must have parked in a different spot."

They watched Manji fold his newspaper and gaze around the square. He walked to the nail trap, hunkered down and touched the points. Manji took off his brown tweed jacket, joined his hands and seemed to be praying.

"What the heck is he at?" Berry whispered as Manji carefully lay on the bed of nails and relaxed in the September sun.

By mid-morning, clumps of spectators hung at street corners and shop doors looking at the reclined foreigner. Manji stayed still during the Angelus and a little while later rose from the bed, stretched himself, tipped his toes. They peered at his back: no sign of blood. Bridgey Looney blessed herself and muttered that as true as God, poor Manji was a saint. Only a very pious being could punish the body so hard and not damage it, she thought.

Coyne the butcher was enraged and said there was only one way to run him out of town: The Gun. Peter Berry flinched and suggested violence might be extreme. He proposed a delegation should approach Manji and fair and square, tell him to leave town.

Coyne disagreed and muttered,

"From my experience, The Gun is the only answer."

While Coyne brooded on using The Gun, the weather changed and winter arrived with little warning. The crows roosted early and night dimmed the town before children were home from school. Manji came every morning and sat in his car, reading and listening to the radio. He stayed until well after dark and left without earning a cent.

Early in November the frost began and a stillness settled on the town. People stayed indoors and the streets were silent. Manji sat in the taxi, starting the engine every so often to heat up the vehicle. For days that was the only sound in town, until a muffled racket started in Upper Clare Street: Rita Kelly and the husband were fighting again. It began on a Tuesday afternoon and continued in bouts and spasms until Friday morning. Then furniture crashed, Rita screamed and glass broke. The town froze as a door banged, its brass knocker clattering home three or four times.

Rita quickly walked down Clare Street carrying a small suitcase. Her husband shouted after her, called her a warping bitch, a rotten gall-bag. She made for the taxi in the square and Manji was out before she reached it. He opened the back door with a bow and a smile for the tearful young woman. The cab quickly turned and took the north road out of town, Manji smiling, nodding his head.

When he didn't return that afternoon, they thought he must have taken her far away. And when Manji didn't show the following day, they reckoned he had taken her further still. By the end of the week, he still hadn't returned and they began to realize that he never would.

"I should have used The Gun," Coyne the butcher muttered, "that fella was only waiting for his chance."

# ELLIE

ELLIE SETTLED INTO A BOOTH IN HARRY'S Diner and looked out the window at the goose-feather snow flakes tumbling down on Columbus, Ohio. Another winter, another year. Lately she began to worry about growing old and alone in America and foresaw a future of empty nights in a warm sitting-room with three yellow canaries for company. It never troubled her before, but this was her first winter without Antonio, the first Christmas she had ever spent all alone. On Christmas night she had wept by the fire when the season crept through the tinsel and the red-berried holly. Jingle bells and radio carols brought her back to the cradle and she cried for home for the first time in decades. But she'd never go back now.

Ellie scanned the menu. Clam chowder: it was a day for soup. Cindy Schultz, daughter of Harry, took her order and complained about the cold and the recession.

"By the way Mrs. Lazurino," she said, "you're Irish, right?" Ellie nodded.

"You know, we've a young girl from Ireland working here now, you guys must meet."

Over soup, Ellie brooded on Ireland. She had heard from Monsignor O'Connor that the youth were leaving in thousands. No change. No future there, nothing but the past. Her own past was there—the worst part of it anyway. No wish to return. The young girl would be better off in America, look how good it had been to Ellie. She arrived with two dollars in her pocket one October Monday and never looked back. She worked hard for everything she got—but at least she got it. She was angry when she arrived and the work occupied her mind and blocked out the horror of the other side. She washed it away with soap and prayers; scrubbing floors by day and laundering clothes by night.

Even after she married Antonio she kept working twelve hours a day, though there was no need to. Poor Antonio was a good husband, the Lord have mercy on him. A thoughtful man who made a fortune from undertaking. He was obsessed with the solemn art of burying the dead and often told her everyone he buried went straight to heaven. He was a staunch Catholic, and so was she, but his faith was greater. Poor Antonio. Never asked about her previous life in Ireland. They never had a family. Antonio wasn't like that. Couldn't couple. But she didn't mind, she wanted a cloistered life.

Straight off the plane, Ellie thought with a smile when she met Stella Murphy, the young Irish waitress. Red hair, big innocent brown eyes, plump rosy cheeks.

"What part of Ireland are you from?" Ellie asked.

"A place called Tubberfola, West Clare."

"Tubberfola?" Ellie repeated, "never heard of it."

"Where are you from yourself?" the girl asked shyly.

"Ballygale," said Ellie, sweetening her coffee with two tiny pills.

"Ballygale near Castlehowley?"

"Yes," Ellie said, "that's the place."

"I know it well!" the girl gushed, "my mother is from there. God but isn't it a small world."

Ellie's cup stopped an inch from her mouth.

"My mother's maiden name was Frawly," continued the girl, delighted to find an Irish soul on a snowy American day, "Her people had a shop near the school. You must know it."

Ellie remembered it but shook her head and said,

"I've been gone a long time honey."

Stella smiled sadly and said

"You should go back for a holiday sometime,"

Ellie shook her head and muttered,

"No honey. I've no wish to."

"What age were you when you left?" Stella asked.

"Your age honey."

"You must know The Phoenix Kelly so—he'd be about your own go."

"Phoenix Kelly? No Phoenix Kelly there in my time."

"You must know him," the girl insisted, "he was a great ladies man. Murt is his proper name."

The name Murt Kelly ruffled Ellie and she looked out at the falling snow.

"The only Murt Kelly I knew from Ballygale is long dead honey," she muttered, with a frown, "may the Lord have mercy on him."

"I bet it's his wife you're thinking of," said Stella, "She was burned to death during the Civil War. That's who you're thinking about...No, Phoenix is alive as you or me."

"Burned to death during the civil war?" Ellie muttered.

"She was only twenty-one or two, Ellie Kelly was her name."

Ellie was stunned.

"We must be thinking of different Kellys," she stammered. She was feeling weak.

"Ah no," said the waitress firmly, "There's only one Murt Kelly—sure his second wife...."

Ellie collapsed in the booth as the words 'second wife' touched her ear drums. Second wife, she swooned with the snow outside. Stella screamed and stared wide-eyed as if she just found a corpse.

When Ellie came around, a young man who looked like a Mormon preacher was holding her hand and a woman in a fur coat passed smelling salts under her nose.

"I'm alright." stammered Ellie, waving them away, "I'll be fine in a second."

"Will I call you a cab Mrs. Lazurino?" Cindy asked nervously.

"Yes," whispered Ellie, "please do."


Ellie came home in a daze, fed the canaries and took out the decanter of Scotch. She half-filled a tumbler with ice and topped it to the brim with whiskey. She crumbled into her green arm-chair and stared at the fire, still bewildered by the news Stella Murphy had imparted. The waitress was the first person with word of Ballygale that Ellie met since she arrived in America, forty years before. She had put the place out of her mind, locked the door and vowed never to return. And now it was as if she was back in the middle of it.

"Jesus Mary an' Joseph," she whispered, "but this couldn't be true. This couldn't be true. Or am I going crazy or something?"

The nightmare broke loose but she hadn't the strength nor the will to stop it. Ellie couldn't even muster up a prayer and relived The Night of the Burning. Black smoke stung her eyes, Hell on Earth. Ballygale, a brooding town torn in two by the Civil War, blood stained streets and burned out houses. A dark town where night came early and idealists fought with bullets and fire. She had been married to an idealist, a marked man who made her a marked woman. He told her it would only be a matter of time until 'they' would get them both and he begged her to leave but she stayed.

And then one night she woke alone in a bedroom full of smoke and heard the rush of flames up the stairs and the crack-crack-crack of gunfire down below. She cried Murt's name and thought she heard him telling her to run, run, run. Screaming prayers she groped up the attic stairs, flames at her heels, her husband swearing and cursing at Christ in the belly of the blaze. It was the prayers that saved her, she later told God, the prayers guided her out the skylight and over slate roofs and red-rust sheds to safe ground at the edge of the town. From Hogan's hay-barn she saw the flames eat through the roof of her house and heard the screams and shouts in the street.

"They're all inside," a man roared.

"Oh Jesus have mercy on them," she heard a woman wail, "get a priest. Get a priest."

Politics, dead patriots and priests. Life cycle of the revolution. Ballygale on a winter's night, the pungent smell of smoke, crackling of a dying fire, shouting in the street, stars in the sky. Ellie pulled a man's trousers from the clothesline in Hogan's yard and fled the town.

After a few whiskeys, she called Monsignor O'Connor, the Irish pastor who lived across the road behind St. Mary's church. From start to finish, her story took more than a half-hour to tell and Monsignor O'Connor changed the receiver from ear to ear many times. He detected from her voice that she had been drinking and wondered for a split-second if she was hallucinating.

"What do you make of it?" Ellie asked finally.

"Well I'm shocked Ellie. Shocked. I mean I never knew you were married in Ireland."

"Nobody did, Monsignor, it didn't matter before. But it's different now—if it's true—I mean if my first husband is alive. That's why I'm calling you. I'm wondering what to do about it."

"If I were you, I'd confirm the facts before I'd do anything," he said firmly. He turned in his swivel chair and gauged the distance to the drinks cabinet.

"That's what I was thinking Monsignor. I s'pose I could contact the local police station—they'd know if it's true. I mean if the Murt the girl was talking about is my Murt."

"Well," said the Monsignor, cleaning a tumbler with his handkerchief, "I wouldn't involve the police at this stage."

He put his hand over the mouthpiece and poured whiskey quietly into the glass.

"You wouldn't?"

"No Ellie. In a small town that could lead to anything. This is too sensitive. It might only complicate things further. It could be embarrassing as well for all concerned—if this Murt Kelly is a different person."

"I see what you mean."

"Ballygale, you said Ellie. What diocese is that in? "

"Dunalla, Monsignor."

"Can you hold on one second until I get a pen..."

He left down the receiver and swallowed the whiskey in one draught, picked up the phone again and said,

"I'm back—Dunalla, that's Kevin Fox's territory—a colleague who was in Rome with me."

"At the Vatican?"

"The Irish College, Ellie. If you like, I can get in contact with Monsignor Fox and maybe he could make a few discreet enquiries for us. But first I'll go and talk to that girl Stella..."

"God that'd be great Monsignor. Thanks a million."

"Not at all Ellie. We're here for more than prayers."

Monsignor O'Connor left down the receiver and sat still for a few seconds, then exhaled slowly and drank another shot of whiskey.

Stella Murphy had been dismissed by the time the priest got to Harry's Diner to check the facts and the clergyman carried a grave look when he met Ellie with the news. But he also brought good tidings: he had telephoned Monsignor Fox who agreed make the enquiries and search church records. Ellie gave her pastor the Kelly family landmarks, the births, deaths and marriages, red letter dates that still glimmered in her mind. He took it all down in neat writing in a small black notebook and promised to get the information to his colleague in Ireland immediately. Ellie poured him a generous glass of Irish whiskey and had tea herself. She wondered what she would do if the story was indeed true but the Monsignor said they'd cross that bridge when they'd come to it.

"But whether it's true or not," she sighed, "it was a terrible shock to get."

"If I were you, Ellie," he advised, "I'd put the whole business out of my mind for the time being. Are you coming to the bingo tomorrow night?"

"I am Monsignor. You're right. The best thing to do is to stop wondering about it altogether. Sure it all might be some kind of a joke or something."

"You never know," he said, thinking how strange it was. In the years he had known Ellie, all she spoke about was her Italian husband and the funeral business in America. And now people were coming back to her from the dead. Just like a tabloid head-line. The Monsignor wiped his brow. God preserve the parish from all harm, he prayed, leaving a thimbleful of whiskey in the glass. He refused all offerings of more drink.

"That's my limit," he protested, rising to his feet.

At the door, she pressed a twenty dollar bill into his hand.

"God Bless you Ellie *astore*," he thanked, "everything will work out grand for you."


The Monsignor held the news from Ellie for almost a week. He paced the parlor, cursed the red haired waitress and only prayed for guidance when he began to hear voices. Spurred by whiskey he arrived at the big green house one frosty evening and broke the story. Yes, he sighed, it seemed her Murt Kelly was alive. The Monsignor read from his black notebook,

"According to the records of Saint Malachy's Church, Ballygale, his first wife, Ellen Bridgit Kelly neé Lowry—is dead and buried in Ballygale. That's you, Ellie..."

"Oh Holy Mother of Divine Jesus...."

"His second wife, Florence Agnes Kelly neé MacMahon is also buried there. Murt or Mortimer Kelly married his third wife, Mary Corless, on June 14, 1939."

Ellie nodded. The Monsignor sighed and put away his book.

"Well that's that," she muttered, backing into an armchair, "That's according to the records."

The Monsignor nodded.

"And I'm supposed to be dead," she said weakly, "but I'm alive."

The clergyman frowned and stared at his fingers. He didn't want to get into any existentialist discussions. Bigamy sirens wailed down the chimney and he curled and flexed his toes.

"What do you make of it at all?" she asked in a wounded voice.

"Well," he said quietly, "this is a very complicated situation —from a church point of view and also from a secular one." He cleared his throat, crossed his legs and continued, "This is a situation where there is no right or wrong. There is no blame Ellie. You both thought each other was dead and you...naturally enough...made new lives for yourselves. Now a lot of water has gone under the bridge in the meantime and the current situation arises."

"And I'm supposed to be dead and buried."

"Yes. According to the church records."

"Buried by a priest."

"I presume so..."

"Wiped off the face of the earth. Gone."

"Well, over there yes, but you're here."

"I see." she said sullenly.

The Monsignor was confident that God would look favorably on the situation and that all would be forgiven.

"Excuse me Monsignor," she challenged, "Forgive who for what? What are you saying? Sure it's all the fault of the church. According to the church, I'm dead and buried."

Ellie was angry and she sprang from the chair and pranced around the sitting room table. She needed a drink but didn't want to offer him one. The church had gotten enough out of her. She wished he would leave. With her back to him, Ellie stood by the bookcase and began to juggle encyclopedias around the shelves. The Monsignor felt her ire.

"Ellie," he said firmly, "I'm sorry to be the bearer of such news, but for God's sake, take it easy. Sit down *a grá*."

Ellie didn't answer, just kept thumping books around until she felt like dumping the lot on top of him. Suddenly she bolted from the room and slammed the door, sent canaries shrieking, feathers and bird seed flying. The Monsignor tapped his knee softly. He heard the clatter in the kitchen. Nonsensical noise. Anger. Frustration. Heartbreak. He sighed, donned hat and coat and left the house quietly.

In two days Ellie lost her faith. The Church had slaved her soul, short changed her out of life. No proper Jesus or Blessed Virgin would stare dead pan, day after day, night after night for forty years, accepting prayers and knowing them to be off target. The prayers didn't even keep Murt on the straight and narrow. Getting married not once but twice after she had departed. The bastard, she spat, sweeping the floor so hard that she felt dizzy and had to sit.

"And me on my knees," she panted, "for the best part of my life, pleading with God that...Murt Kelly could get to heaven ...and he...hoppin' in an' out'a bed with every bitch in the country. The dirty bastard."

She had thought life would begin again in Heaven and God alone knew how much she wanted Murt Kelly to be there too. That was the vision that kept her alive: that some sunny day she would meet him there. She used picture the scene in her prayers—she'd be walking along a bright road that went from one heavenly town to another, in the company of an angel or a saint and then they'd meet Murt Kelly. He would look the same as the first time she met him, black wavy hair, soft face and pogish grin. But now she saw two other women with him. Ellie wept and her tears washed away years of hope. In blind anger she doused the fire with holy water and vowed never to talk to God again.

Monsignor O'Connor dropped by a few evenings later with a half-pound of Irish breakfast tea. Ellie was courteous and ushered him into the sitting room where she had a smoking fire and clouds of smuts. He thought she looked bedraggled and it struck him that she might be drinking when he saw the untidiness of the room. Newspapers scattered on the floor, cups on the mantelpiece, a greasy dinner plate or two behind her armchair, television a little too loud. After five minutes or so of small talk, the Monsignor cleared his throat and said,

"Ellie, I was thinking about your situation in regard to what we heard from Ireland..."

He sighed, pursed his lips and said gravely, "In my opinion, the best thing to do is to forget about it."

"Forget about it?"

"Let sleeping dogs lie as they say. Forget about it as if it never happened."

"Well of course it never happened." Ellie said, "I mean—I never died and he never died."

The Monsignor frowned, but knew better than to voice his opinion. He nodded instead and said softly,

"You know, a situation like this could turn out very complicated, very complicated—for us all."

Ellie glanced at him, wondering whether to cross swords or not.

"It's complicated already Monsignor," she pointed.

Monsignor O'Connor nodded, his heart thumped and he prayed to the beat. He prayed that God and all the Saints in Heaven would bring Ellie to his way of thinking, guide her out of the minefield. He said,

"I know the whole affair has been a terrible shock to you, but God is good."

"A terrible blow to get after forty years," Ellie muttered.

There was silence for a while and then she whispered,

"But maybe the best thing to do is to offer it up to Our Lady of Fatima."

He flinched with surprise. Thank God, he thought, she has come to her senses.

"You're a great woman Ellie," the Monsignor said, genuine emotion in his voice, "God will have a special place in Heaven for you."

Fifteen minutes later he stepped out of the green house like a frisky poodle. His prayers were answered and Ellie was detoured around multiple counts of bigamy, church hearings, paperwork, scandal—the works.

"God will have a special place in Heaven for you," she mimicked, watching him cross the road to the church. How dare he pay her off with the promise of a special place in Heaven. She knew there was no Heaven.

A month or so later in Ballygale, Phoenix Kelly was in bed with a hangover when his wife Mary brought him the mail and thumped back to the shop without a word. The blues again, Phoenix sighed and panned the letters. Envelopes with windows —bills, bills, bills. A postcard from Lourdes, three letters from the County Council planning department and the plump letter from America. He frowned at the sender's address sticker, a tiny decal of the Stars and Stripes—Mrs. E. T. Lazurino. Someone who wants to trace ancestors, he thought, settled his spectacles and opened the airmail.

Ellie wrote:

'*Dear Murt, brace yourself because what I write will shock you...*'

Phoenix stopped reading and quickly turned to the last page of the letter—two old photographs fell from the sheaf but he ignored them and stared at the writer's signature. Ellie Lazurino neé Lowry.

"Who the fuck is this?" he muttered, blood pumping to his head.

Then he looked at the photographs. Ellie, straight from the Thirties, standing beside a table in one, by a long black hearse in the other. Phoenix froze and stared at them for a long time. He trembled through the letter, thought he'd get sick, went to the bathroom and read it twice over again. Went up to the attic and looked at the photographs under the skylight. Ellie, short brown wavy hair, dark eyes and almond face.

His headache tightened. He was stumped, bewildered for the

first time in years. He looked around the attic, not sure he was alone, and read the letter again, fighting away voices from the past.

"Jesus Christ," he whispered, "this is crazy...this is bananas."

Phoenix went out the back door and hurried up the lane to Bridgey Looney's bar. He felt safe there, it was an old nationalist's shrine. Bridgey's husband Miko had been killed in the War, but she never re-married. Phoenix looked pale and Bridgey asked if he had been sick. The eyes were giving trouble, he said and ordered a brandy. Could be the wind, she offered, wind affected the eyes at this time of the year. Phoenix sniffled and looked at himself in the mirror behind the bar. Bridgey gathered he was in no mood for chat and returned to the kitchen.

Phoenix fingered the letter in his pocket and shivered. It was all too shocking to be false. Just like she said she was shocked out of her wits to hear that he was alive. The photographs clenched it. The soft serene smile. And her ankles. Down the years he often thought of her ankles, slender and smooth. How does she look now? Would she know him if they met. He was shaking, sweating. Oh dear Jesus, this is bats. The woman on whose death he built a political dynasty was returning to haunt him. But maybe somebody was having him on. They did strange things in America. Blackmail? He tapped the counter for another drink and Mrs. Looney came from the kitchen.

"Same again, please Bridgey,"

"Alright. Are you feelin' any better Phoenix?"

"Not much Bridgey,"

"You poor cratur," she muttered, serving his brandy, "Will you try a Goldflake?" she asked, offering him a cigarette.

"No thanks Bridgey. No, no."

She wondered what was bothering him. He looks tormented, Bridgey thought, maybe it's the taxman.

Phoenix was imagining the scenario if Ellie returned to Ballygale. Resurrection of the woman whose brutal death was celebrated in song and legend. The local golf club bore her name, as did the football field, the new housing estate and girls school. Ellie Kelly was a heroine. They had a plaque erected to her memory at the site of the old house. What would he do? What would his family say? Uproar.

As if picking up his thoughts, Bridgey sighed,

"Ah there's very few of the old crowd left now."

She looked out the window at the run-down town and reminisced about the old days. They were always fighting on for the bright new day, she whispered, but what came could never match the old ones.

"Give me another brandy please Bridgey," he said shakily.

Phoenix brought a bottle home and drank in the attic until his wife Mary went to the church. Then he called his son Patrick, the Senator. The old man was drunk and rambled on the phone. Can this wait, Patrick interrupted, I'm about to leave for Dublin, the Senate sits in the morning. I wouldn't be calling you if it could, Phoenix slurred, I want you here in ten minutes.

Patrick charged into the house like a bull.

"Well," he grunted, "what's up?"

"Get a drink and sit down," said his father.

A few minutes into  the story, Patrick sprang to his feet and shouted,

"This is ridiculous!"

"But it's true," Phoenix nodded.

"No, no," argued Patrick, "it's not the story. It's you. You've gone stark raving fucking mad from drink."

"Sit down and shut up!" ordered Phoenix.

Patrick mopped his brow, lit a cigarette. Phoenix told his son he had never seen Ellie's remains, being in hospital with burns and gun shot wounds when she was laid to rest. Anyway, they said the body found in the debris was burned beyond recognition...

"Look," Patrick cut in, "Ellie Kelly is dead. Dead, dead, dead. And the trouble is, you never came to grips with that fact."

Phoenix raised his hand to interrupt his son,

"Let me continue," over-ruled the Senator, "and now it's all catching up on you. It's driving you to drink and drink is driving you fucking mad."

Phoenix shook his head and shouted,

"No, no, you're not hearing me. This is serious..."

"It's you who's not hearing me. Mama says you're drinking day and night. For Christ's sake man pull yourself together. Look at you! You're...you're like someone out of the fucking nut-house."

Phoenix stared bleary eyed at his son, the man he coached and groomed for politics.

"Fuck off to your Free State Senate," he mumbled and staggered upstairs to the attic.

Phoenix drank all the following day and the day after that again. Patrick called from the Senate every few hours but the old man was either out of the house or out of his mind with drink. He talked with his mother about getting Phoenix admitted to a private psychiatric hospital. Lock him up until he came to his senses. And do it quick before he disgraces us all.

After the fifth day of the binge, Mary bawled Phoenix out, screaming that he was a lunatic, a drunk, a womanizer, a useless sod. Exasperated, she took his clothes and shoes and went to lock them in the back room. He could crawl to the pub in his drawers she fumed. She searched his pockets, took his check book, snooped through his wallet, emptied it, dug deeper into the pockets and found the letter from America.

The doctor said Mary Kelly died of natural causes: her heart stopped. Phoenix was floored and Patrick went to pieces. The funeral was huge, long black government Mercedes nosed behind each other like crocodiles and ten priests and a bishop laid her to rest. The mourners said her death would bury Phoenix, there was nothing now between him and the bottle.

Monsignor O'Connor saw the estate agent's sign going up on Ellie's lawn and hurried across the road.

"Come in Monsignor," she said, "I was just going to call you."

"Ellie," he said with surprise, "you're selling the house."

"I am...too big for me Monsignor. Too big."

"And where're you moving to?"

"Florida," she said, throwing him a red herring, "I'm going to the sunshine. The weather here is very harsh Monsignor. Would you like a drop of tea."

"Just a cup in my hand. Great God this comes as a complete shock to me."

"It's a good time to sell," Ellie said, walking away from him, "and a good time to move. I'll be settled in before I know it."

"I still can't believe it," the pastor said, following her around the kitchen like a toddler, "Ellie, you're not thinking about going to Ireland? Are you?"

"Well as sure as I'm standing here," she swore, "not in a million years."

He squinted at the brochures for retirement villages scattered on the coffee table. Pictures of swimming pools, seniors on golf-mobiles, seniors playing tennis, seniors dancing under dim lights.

"Well I don't know what to say," he sighed, "isn't this all very sudden Ellie?"

"If I don't do it now, I'll never do it."

Ellie sold her house on a Tuesday and a furniture buyer came by next day and offered her pittance for the contents. Take it or leave it, he said, let me know tomorrow. She expected someone from the bird fanciers club to call at four o' clock about the canaries and all afternoon she lingered by the cages holding back tears. The doorbell chimed and the birds burst into glorious song. Heavenly rolls, twirls, chirps and triplets.

"Mrs. Lazurino?" the grey haired man asked softly.

"Yes," she said.

"I'm Murt Kelly."

"Oh Jesus!" she gasped, "Murt!"

They met with open arms. Re-united lovers, their tears mingled. He caressed her head and forty years melted away in seconds.

"Ellie my darling," he whispered.

"Ah Murt," she wept, "I knew you wouldn't let me down. Come in, come in and close the door."

# JOURNEYMEN

MY MUSIC CAREER BEGAN THE YEAR I joined Mickey Moran's Country and Oldtime Stars. I was seventeen, had long hair and played electric guitar, one of the solid red axes like Keith Richards had. Good for the image, Mickey said. There were four of us in the 'outfit', as he called it: himself played a piano accordion, Tats was on the drums, me on guitar and Tony Flynn covered clarinet, flute, maracas and tambourine. Mickey did the vocals and encouraged singers from the floor.

That summer, we had a residency in The Springs Hotel, a ghost of a place that had been closed for about forty years, until a nephew of the owner came home from England in a shimmering black suit and decided to put the clock back. He brushed away the cobwebs, swept the floors and opened the doors: everything else was the same as the day it closed, maybe even the drink. The place had an eerie feeling about it, like a Frankenstein movie set. Dim chandeliers and dank carpets, huge wall mirrors, long velvet burgundy curtains, weighed down with dust. Shadows everywhere, strange people passing through, like they were searching for their youth.

The bandstand was in the lounge, a long narrow brownish room with a bar inside the door. It had a large dance floor with chairs and tables strung along side walls under tall gilded mirrors. The Springs took a long time to warm up and only got going when the hot spots down town bubbled over. By then, half the band were drunk. This was my introduction to another side of life after school: steamy dancing, free whiskey, untipped cigarettes and the girls in short skirts who sat near the stage. Life became a minefield of possibilities.

The oddest things happened in The Springs. One night just as the crowd were loosening up, a bat flew into the lounge and half the women in the place and all the men with toupees went hysterical. We played a waltz and Mickey asked for calm while the nephew, full on, tried to catch the creature with a child's shrimp net. Bottles broke, chairs crashed, tables overturned. But we played on, smiling that everything was ace.

Another night, an elf of a man in a pastor's grey suit danced into the hall embracing a live-sized cardboard cut-out nurse. She held an Irish Sweepstake ticket aloft in her hand and I'll never forget the way she smiled over his shoulder as they wheeled by the bandstand. Then there was the night the cops arrived, a dozen or more, running like troopers, looking for a weightlifter from East Clare who had overturned a chip van in the square. One of the lawmen fell out of rank and hung on at the bar. Sans hat and tunic, he lashed back gin and tonic and at four in the morning when everyone was yawning he did an Elvis impersonation: "Crying in the Chapel", "Wooden Heart", "Blue Suede Shoes". Eyes closed in ecstasy, while Tats did a drum solo, he jived off the stage and went to hospital with a broken leg.

The final night we performed in The Springs, the place was totally empty. Nobody there. It was the weekend after the Listowel races and the crowd had gone to boogie elsewhere. The party was over, Winter was slicing in and all the sinners had flown. The night was brutally wet and windy and there was a cold blue light on the street. Most other places had closed, but the nephew wanted to go down with the ship. And so he did, keeping himself busy by filling drinks for the band and bringing them to the stage. Have one himself, then another round for the band. I had forsaken bottled beer by this time and was maturely supping shots of vodka with a dash of red lemonade. On we played, windows rattling, breeze whistling through the cracks.

Sometime later, a hippy lady who had a caravan outside the town traipsed into the lounge, black dog behind her. After a couple of pints she came up and sang Marianne Faithful songs with us. Then the nephew invited her to dance and Mickey slowed down the tempo to a crawl. After another few numbers, the nephew and the hippy were kissing under a fly spattered chandelier, while Tony Flynn warbled "Stranger on the Shore" on clarinet. Vintage stuff. Tats drunkenly tapped along on drums and Mickey and myself vamped blue chords to fill the gaps.

Before taking his dance partner off to more private quarters, the nephew told us to help ourselves at the bar and lock the door behind us when we were going home. We played the national anthem, drum rolls and all, to an empty hall and at half-past midnight, took up positions at the bar. Mickey asked what we were having and God alone knows what we drank.

At some late hour, I remember being outside, black rain pelting down from heaven, trees groaning in the wind. Tats trying to lock the hotel door and catching the hem of his coat in it. Tony Flynn standing on the lawn, crooning "Blue Moon" towards the only lit window in The Springs. Mickey shouting at us to get into the car.

We proceeded out of town with the utmost caution, took the unapproved way home and got lost. Mickey drove around boreens and bog roads until we ran out of petrol in the middle of nowhere. There we sat in the pitch-black, smoking cigarettes, drinking whiskey from a bottle Tats found in his coat pocket. Waiting for daylight, wondering where we were, freezing cold, deafened by the rain dancing on the car roof. Tats muttering,

"The road downhill was an easy one, and that's the one we took."

# OUT OF THE BLUE

THE TELEGRAM CAME TO INISRIGGLE ISLAND
post office, directed to nobody in particular—

Bridey Mullet died in Chicago. STOP.
Remains arriving at Shannon airport Friday
January 12. STOP.

"The Lord have mercy on her soul," sighed
Paddy Rodgers the postmaster, block lettering the
news on a telegram form. Bridey Mullet. No
addressee. He lit a cigarette and wondered who he
should deliver the blow to.

There were five families of Mullets on the
island and he knew they all had somebody in
America. Start at the top, he thought, first lay it
on the most important Mullet: Mouse Mullet, the
headmaster. The ideal man, inhaled Paddy. Plus,
in the absence of priests and police, Mouse was
the community overseer, representative of church
and state, he would know what to do. Even if the
problem wasn't his, he might adopt it. Paddy slipped
the telegram into an official green envelope and
sealed the shock. Then he waddled to the kitchen
and announced to his wife,

"Bridey Mullet died in Chicago and her remains are arriving at Shannon airport on Friday."

"The Lord have mercy on her," Biddy blurted, blessed herself and eased into a fireside chair. She offered up a prayer for the dead while Paddy bit his lower lip and fanned his face with the telegram.

"Was she a young woman?" his wife whispered.

"About sixty-five," guessed Paddy.

"The heart I s'pose," she sighed.

"She was run over by a train," he said solemnly.

"Oh Holy Mother of Jesus!" jolted Biddy.

"The Lord have mercy on her," muttered Paddy, buttoning his black oilskin coat. He pulled a red and blue knitted pixi cap over his head, stepped out into the chilly January afternoon and headed for the school.

There was a gale blowing. The weathermen got that part of it right, Paddy thought, Force Seven at least. His nose ran. Pellets of rain stung his cheeks and battered the oilskin coat, but he hardly noticed, he was wondering about Bridey Mullet. He couldn't place any Bridey Mullet at the age he pictured her: sixty-five. About Biddy's age. That's what came to him as he wrote out the telegram and he was seldom wrong about these things. Paddy believed he had a Gift, though he wouldn't go as far as thinking it was Second Sight. He could just pick up latent signals from the wire.

When he opened the school door the wind raged into the hall and trashed the place in one gust, blowing notices and papers into a cockfight. It took him a couple of charges to shoulder the door shut against the gale. Then a classroom door burst open and Mouse dashed out.

"Paddy!" he said with surprise.

"Sorry to bother you Master Mullet, but a telegram just came from America...and it's addressed to nobody."

"A telegram addressed to nobody...come in Paddy."

The classroom was empty and warm with the smell of cigarettes and turf smoke. Paddy also got the whiff of whiskey and said,

"You let them home early."

"There's a bad gale promised," said Mouse, stoking up the fireplace under the blackboard. Sparks showered on the floor and the teacher stamped them out asking,

"Good or bad news Paddy?"

"Kinda lonesome news, and there's a Mullet connection," he forewarned, sliding the green envelope from an inside pocket and biting his lower lip.

Mouse frowned: Lonesome news addressed to nobody, but it had a Mullet connection.

"Will I give it to you?" Paddy asked apologetically.

Mouse nodded. The postmaster handed him the envelope and backed away.

"I hate telegrams," muttered Mouse, "I hate fucking telegrams."

He stared at the news and Paddy saw his lips move and could hear him whisper,

"Who in the name of Jesus is Bridey Mullet?"

"What do you make of it?" ventured the postmaster.

"I don't know any Bridey Mullet," he said slowly.

"I s'pose she must be related to someone here if she coming here to be buried," Paddy said.

"Remains are arriving in Shannon on Friday," the Mouse muttered.

He dreaded funerals, hated the darkness, the suspension of all activities and the constant wailing of the Roche Sisters who roamed the island visiting haunts of the deceased, mourning and keening like tom cats until the corpse was buried a week. Wakes and funerals spun him into drunkenness and depression, a sympathetic death with the departed soul.

"She might be some relation to Johnny Fox Peter," Mouse suggested, "he had someone in Chicago. I'd say he's your best bet."

He passed the telegram back to Paddy and offered him a cigarette.

Johnny Fox Peter Mullet was an island oddball. A lean heron-like man in late middle-age, strange behavior hit him every now and then like a virus. Soft in the head, was the islanders' term for his condition. One month he might be Saint Jude, next month his normal self and the following month he could be John Wayne. They said the moon influenced him; that and drink. The postmaster raised his eyes to heaven. Since Christmas Johnny was Manann MacLear, the pagan god who the old people said controlled the weather. Fox boasted he had turned the elements against the world and would keep the pressure up until the County Council sanctioned his grant for a new bathroom.

Johnny Fox Peter's wife opened the door an inch or two. She freaked when Paddy mentioned the word 'telegram' and banged the door in his face. He heard her bolt it.

"Shag off outa here," she shouted, kicking the door from the inside, "shag off outa here, yourself and your telegram, going around the island frightening the life outa people. Shag off outa here."

"I'm only doin' my duty," apologized Paddy, slipping the telegram under the door.

Tuesday evening is dark at five and there's boiled eggs and brown bread for tea in the posthouse. On the radio a man talks about worms in cattle and Biddy wonders about Bridey Mullet and the train. She hears sirens and sees blood on the tracks and swarms of people running and praying. When the phone rings she snaps from her daydream, leaves the station in Chicago and chirps,

"Inisriggle postoffice."

"Father Looney please."

It was Johnny Fox Peter's son, Brian, ringing from the kiosk outside the post office door, calling the priest on the mainland. She peeped through the curtains: Johnny and the wife crushed in the box, Brian stood outside in the wind and rain, receiver to his ear.

"Insert ten pence please caller," Biddy said.

"Put in the money!" ordered Brian, handing the phone to his father.

Johnny Fox Peter told the priest that his uncle's daughter had died in Chicago and was being brought back to Inisriggle for burial. The priest sympathized with him and asked what the arrangements were. Fox said remains were arriving at Shannon on Friday and Father Looney suggested Sunday might be a good day to inter her, when he'd be over to say Mass and hear confessions. Of course it all depended on the weather, he added. Don't worry about the weather Father, Johnny Fox Peter said, I'll fix the weather.

"That poor woman of the Mullet's is being buried after Mass on Sunday," said Biddy when she returned to the kitchen, "she's some relation to Johnny Fox Peter."

"The Lord have mercy on her," muttered Paddy, relieved that the telegram found the right home. He turned up the radio to hear the weather forecast: another gale warning, Force Six to Seven.

"Fox said he's going to fix the weather," Biddy chuckled.

"If he's not careful," drawled Paddy, "the weather might fix him."

By noon next day, everyone on the island knew about the Mullet woman who had died in America. Johnny Fox Peter was drowning his sorrow in the pub and men slipped in and out to shake his hand and have a drink with him. She was only thirty-nine, he told them, and she had a big job in the government and owned three houses in Chicago. She had neither kith nor kin, nobody in the world but the Fox Peters on Inisriggle. Bridey Mullet had contracted a fatal disease, he said, and her dying wish was to be buried in Inisriggle beside her grandfather and grandmother.

Mouse Mullet helped with the funeral arrangements and organized an undertaker on the mainland to pick up the remains at the airport and take them to the harbor in Ballyline. Johnny tried to settle the weather so the mail boat would ferry Father Looney and the coffin across on Sunday morning. Not a chance. On that morning the island was hurricane whipped and people wouldn't go outside the door for fear of being blown away. It was noon before Johnny Fox Peter ventured out. Lugging a kite and a battery, he set off for the top of the island to work Ben Franklin's experiment in reverse: fly the kite and charge the sky via the battery. This energy would neutralize the storm, he calculated. But the wind was so strong it whipped kite and battery from his grip and blew them away towards America.

Mouse was sitting by the fire in Harney's pub, sipping a whiskey when Johnny Fox was blown through the door like a sheet of newspaper. The bereaved man was pale as a ghost, God told me to fuck off, he muttered. Mouse bought him a drink and tried to comfort him.

Paddy Rodgers answered in the telephone exchange when Mouse called from Harney's pub.

"How're you Paddy, could you get me Senator Tot McDuil in Castletown. I think the number is four-five."

Tot McDuil listened to Mouse's tale of woe: corpse arrived from America, family distraught because it can't be brought the final leg of the journey, from the mainland to the island. Was there any chance Senator McDuil could arrange for the coast-guard helicopter to ferry a coffin the six miles off shore, as soon as there was a break in the weather. It would be seen as a government friendly gesture to an ignored island and a moving way to bury a lost daughter of the homeland. Mouse suggested Tot come over as well, the priest could also travel over with them. Kill a flock of birds with the one stone. The politician thought it was a great idea. He loved funerals and said he'd see what could be done.

"Tot McDuil is coming over for the funeral of that Mullet woman as soon as the weather settles. They're coming by helicopter," Paddy told his wife that evening over a tea of beans and toast.

"She must be a big shot," Biddy said, "the Lord have mercy on her."

On Tuesday morning early, there was a call from the mainland to say the coastguard helicopter was on standby. Winds were expected to abate around noon and the pilot would make a dash across the six miles of grey water. Tot McDuil and Father Looney would be travelling too. Mouse got word around the island like wild fire: remains arriving by helicopter at noon.

Johnny Fox Peter looked the pallor of death. A scarecrow in black suit, crooked mourning tie and dark tweed cap, he hadn't eaten for a week and his stomach wriggled like a bag of ferrets. He swore he'd never drink again once this funeral was over. His wife wore a black shawl and clutched a pair of Rosary beads as she sniffled around the house, glancing out the window at the sky every couple of minutes. Their son Brian, in blue dancing suit, sat by the fire, his back to both parents. He smoked an untipped cigarette and wondered how much did the dead Yank leave them: at least enough for a motor bike and a color television. Maybe she even left them the houses in Chicago and he'd have to go over there and keep an eye on the property. He might get a wife, a tall blonde. A six-foot Madonna.

Knock on the door. Mouse Mullet dashes in to say it's time to go to the strand where the flying hearse would land. Mrs. Fox Peter began wailing like a banshee, the dreaded moment had arrived: their show, their dead. All eyes and attention, sympathy and pity would be with them. The bereaved Fox Peters. Time for anesthetics. Mouse slipped a bottle from his overcoat pocket and asked for four mugs. Potcheen, the hoi poli of moonshine. Big measures to warm their stomachs and soothe the nerves. Down the hatch. Herself protested, but Johnny and Mouse had another swig and left the house with a shuffle in their step. The son followed behind linking his distraught mother down the sand-blown road to the shore.

It was a grey day and the wind had blown itself out, apart from short gusts that spat rain every ten minutes or so. On the strand it was ice cold and the crowd huddled closer for warmth while they waited for the helicopter. Johnny Fox Peter and family were in the front row, flanked on either side by Mouse Mullet and Harney the publican. It was a miserable wait and they strained their ears for the chopper.

Half an hour passed and the crowd began to murmur: the

wind was picking up again. The moonshine was wearing thin and Johnny Fox Peter was getting grumpy and edgy. Then his wife came up trumps by announcing they should say a decade of the Rosary and led the islanders into a high-pitched mantra. Eerie prayer blown by the wind through holes in stone walls.

When they heard the chopper, prayers became more zealous. God was on their side. The white machine grew bigger and bigger; they could see the coffin dangling underneath and blessed themselves at the sight because no corpse had ever come home like this before.

But the closer the chopper came, the more they noticed the coffin wasn't just dangling: it was swinging, really swinging, like a mad pendulum. Something's wrong, jolted Paddy the postmaster. The wind charged in rapid gusts and the helicopter began jerking and lurching, pulled this way and that by the flying coffin and the elements. On board, Father Looney felt the tug of God and fingered his Holy Water bottle. Senator McDuil was already waving at the crowd on the beach, even though they were at least a thousand strokes away. The pilot apologized for the rocky ride and said they were almost there.

Father Looney muttered Jesus, when the helicopter lost control, spun around suddenly and spiraled downwards. He heard the engine scream and splutter, saw the white wave-tops stream past the windscreen like suds in a washing machine. His head got dizzy,

"Our Father," he cried, "who art in Heaven..."

The pilot was shouting Mayday, Tot McDuil ordered him to do something, do anything.

The crowd on the beach dropped to their knees in screaming prayer. Death in slow motion. Johnny Fox Peter couldn't handle it and ran towards the water, yelling in the old language, waving his hands at the impending doom. He became Moses. Tears streamed down his face and he curled in two and hurled a most primeval scream at whoever was in control of this mess. The island electrified and for a split second, heaven and hell collided.

Afterwards some said they saw lightening strike the coffin before it exploded feet above the water and the helicopter shot to heaven in a ball of flame and was never seen again. More say lightening hit the helicopter first and that Father Looney, Tot McDuil and the pilot were nuked to cinders. Anyway, they were never seen again.

But everyone saw the coffin burst apart and saw a body tumble into the water. The island screamed at the horror. Johnny Fox Peter cried No! No! No! His wife screeched. The son was stunned and looked at the waves. The Roche Sisters keened their deadliest laments and Mouse wet his pants.

Like a sigh from God, rain came and showered pellets of hard water on the islanders. They dispersed, ran helter-skelter to the shelter of their homes, shouting, screaming, wailing. Paddy Rodgers sprinted to his phone, he'd have to notify the mainland about the tragedy. More lightening. Hard rain falling by the bucket. Distant peals of thunder darkened the sky and the sea. It looked like the end of the world.

Mouse linked Johnny Fox Peter and his wife and rushed them home. The son stood on the strand, soaking in the rain, staring at the spot in space where it all happened. He could see debris bobbing around. Jesus Christ, there was a body somewhere out there, maybe three or four bodies. His family would be blamed for the whole tragedy, branded for ever after, as if life on this God forsaken fucking island wasn't bad enough, with his father's fits of madness.

He crouched on the sand and cuddled his head in his arms.

He prayed out of frustration, and pleaded with God, admitting that though he was no saint, and all the family were screwed-up in one way or another, they deserved better than this.

"Even dogs have their day," he told God, "why not us? Why had you to ruin the whole fucking funeral on us and make a right show of us in front of the whole island? Why? Can you answer me that?"

For the first time in his life Brian had a one-to-one chat with God and laid it out straight. He wasn't going to work on Yahwee's farm no more. If the supreme being didn't come up with some retribution for the funeral fiasco, he was quitting. He gave it hot and heavy to God, hinting about the houses in Chicago, the color television and the motorbike. And while He was on their case, God might check on that grant application for a new bathroom that they had submitted months ago to the County Council. Then he went silent while God digested what he had said.

Suddenly a sheet of lightening bounced off the waves with a loud crackle and sizzle and lit the sky like a flash bulb. Brian looked up and a peal of thunder slapped him in the face and fused his mind.

It was dark when the storm passed and Brian sat on the sand, head zinging. He could see the mainland lights twinkling, beckoning. The sea was calmer and the waves were quieter, almost laid back. Debris from the coffin and the body would probably be washed up by morning. There would be cops coming to the island, maybe television people, newspaper reporters. The place would be crawling with questions. His father and mother would make absolute asses of themselves. Maybe they'd be taken away, blamed for the whole disaster and locked up for all time in some asylum.

He walked to the water's edge, thinking he saw something floating close to shore, something pale against the black sea. He looked at the surf, saw a hand rise from the water and his heart thumped at the sight of the dead. He blessed himself. Then he saw a face and heard a woman's voice, calling from the waves. Bridey Mullet. Jesus Christ, he gulped, and ran like hell.

When he had gone sixty feet or so, Brian slowed down and looked back.

"Help me you fool!" he heard and saw a woman threshing out of the tide and falling face down on the damp sand.

Cautiously he walked towards her, thinking she might be a mermaid. But no, she was an American, about his own age, thirty or there abouts. Disorientated. Distraught.

"Do you know what it's like spending eternity in a coffin?" she panted as he wrapped his wet coat around her shivering body.

"I do, I do," he said, helping her home to his father's house.


And that's the way Brandy Shotwell arrived on Inisriggle Island and became Brenda Mullet, wife of Brian Johnny Fox Peter. She laid low for a few months, never venturing outside the door while all the investigation to the Bridey Mullet affair was going on. Not even Mouse Mullet or Paddy Rodgers the postmaster knew she was on the island.

And then one Friday night, she went up to the pub with Brian and shocked the premises into silence. She was the finest lady they had ever seen and knew immediately that a woman like her could only arrive Out of the Blue.

Lightning Source UK Ltd.
Milton Keynes UK
UKOW02f1930150716

278510UK00001B/29/P

9 781930 579132